When the Tripods Came

Books by John Christopher

THE TRIPOD SERIES
When the Tripods Came
The White Mountains
The City of Gold and Lead
The Pool of Fire

THE SWORD TRILOGY
The Prince in Waiting
Beyond the Burning Lands
The Sword of the Spirits

THE FIREBALL TRILOGY
Fireball
New Found Land
Dragon Dance

The Lotus Caves
The Guardians
Dom and Va
Wild Jack
Empty World

When the Tripods Came

JOHN CHRISTOPHER

E. P. DUTTON ⊙ NEW YORK

Library of Congress Cataloging-in-Publication Data
Christopher, John.
    When the Tripods came/by John Christopher.—1st ed.
    p.   cm.—(The Tripod series)
    Summary: Fourteen-year-old Laurie and his family attempt to
flee England when the Tripods descend from outer space and
begin brainwashing everyone with their hypnotic Caps.
    ISBN 0-525-44397-5
    [1. Science fiction.]   I. Title.   II. Series: Christopher,
John. Tripod series.   88-478
        PZ7.C457Wg   1988   CIP
        [Fic]—dc19   AC

Published in the United States by
E. P. Dutton, a division of
Penguin Books USA Inc.

Published simultaneously in Canada by
Fitzhenry & Whiteside Limited, Toronto

Editor: Ann Durell   Designer: Alice Lee Groton
Printed in the U.S.A.   COBE   First Edition
10 9 8 7 6 5 4

to Ben with love

◎ ◎ ◎
ONE

An explosion of noise woke me. It sounded as if a dozen express trains were about to hit the shed. I rolled over in my blanket, trying to get out of the way, and was aware of a blaze of orange, lighting up boxes and bits of old farm equipment and tackle. An ancient rusting tractor looked briefly like an over-grown insect.

"What was that, Laurie?" Andy asked. I could see him sitting up, between me and the window.

"I don't know."

Both light and sound faded and died. A dog started barking—deep-throated, a Labrador maybe. I got up and walked to the window, banging my shin on something in the dark. It was dark outside, too, moon and stars hidden by cloud. A light came on in the farmhouse, which was a couple of hundred me-ters away, just below the ridge.

I said, "It's not raining. What *was* it?"

"Didn't someone at the camp say something about an artillery range on the moor?"

"Nowhere near here, though."

"Whatever they were firing could have gone astray."

Rubbing my shin, I said, "It didn't sound like a shell. And a shell wouldn't produce fireworks like that."

"A rocket, maybe." He yawned loudly. "It's all quiet now, anyway. No sweat. Go to sleep. We've a long trek in the morning."

I stood by the window for a while. Eventually the light in the house went out: the farmer presumably took the same view as Andy. In the pitch black I felt my way to the pile of straw which served as a bed. This was less fun than it had seemed the previous evening; there was little protection from the hardness of the earth floor, and once awake I knew all about the aches in my muscles.

Andy was already asleep. I blamed him for our being here—for volunteering us into the orienteering expedition in the first place, and then for insisting on a left fork which had taken us miles out of our way. It had looked as though we would have to spend the night on the moor, but we'd come across this isolated farm as dusk was thickening. The rules were not to ask for help, so we'd settled down in the shed.

I thought my aches, and resenting Andy, would keep me awake, but I was dead tired. We had set out early from summer camp, and it had been a long day's slog. Drifting into sleep again, I was half aware of another explosion, but it was a distant one, and I was too weary really to wake up—I couldn't even be sure I wasn't dreaming.

Andy woke me with the gray light of dawn filtering in. He said, "Listen."

"What?"

"Listen!"

I struggled into wakefulness. The noise was coming from the direction of the farmhouse, but further away, a succession of loud thumpings, heavy and mechanical.

"Farm machinery?" I suggested.

"I don't think so."

Listening more carefully, I didn't either. The thumps came at intervals of a second or less, and they were getting nearer. There was even a sensation of the ground shaking under me.

"Something heading this way," Andy said. "Something big, by the sound of it."

We crowded together at the small window of the shed. The sun hadn't risen, but to the east the farmhouse was outlined against a pearly sky. Smoke from a chimney rose almost straight: farmers were early risers. It looked like a good day for the trek back to camp. Then I saw what was coming into view on the other side of the house.

The top appeared first, an enormous gray-green hemispherical capsule, flat side down, which seemed to be floating ponderously in midair. But it wasn't floating: a weird stiltlike leg moved in a vast arc across the sky and planted itself just to the right of the farmhouse. As it crashed down a second leg appeared, passing over the house and landing between it and the shed. I could see a third leg, too, which if it followed suit would come to ground close to us, if not on top of us. But at that point, it stopped. The gigantic object, more than twenty meters high, stood straddling the house.

A band of bright green glassy panels ran horizontally along the side of the capsule. It produced an effect that was a cross between multiple staring eyes and a grinning mouth. It wasn't a pleasant grin.

"Someone's making a film." Andy's voice was unsteady. I turned to him and he looked as scared as I felt. "That must be it. A science-fiction movie."

"So where are the cameras?" I felt my voice was coming out wrong, too.

"They probably have to get it into position first."

I didn't know whether he believed it. I didn't.

Something was moving beneath the capsule, curling and twisting and stretching out. It was like an elephant's trunk, or a snake, except that it was silvery and metallic. It corkscrewed down towards the roof of the house and brushed lightly against it. Then it moved to the chimney stack and grasped it with a curling tip. Bricks sprayed like confetti, and we heard them crashing onto the slates.

I was shivering. Inside the house a woman screamed. A door at the back burst open, and a man

4

in shirt and trousers came out. He stared up at the machine looming above him and started running. Immediately a second tentacle uncurled, this time fast and purposeful. The tip caught him before he'd gone ten meters, fastened round his waist, and plucked him from the ground. He was screaming, too, now.

The tentacle lifted him up in front of the row of panels, and his screams turned to muffled groaning. After a few moments the tentacle twisted back on itself. A lenslike opening appeared at the base of the capsule; it carried him towards it and thrust him through. I thought of someone holding a morsel of food on a fork before popping it into his mouth, and felt sick.

His groans ended as the tentacle withdrew, and the opening closed. The woman in the house had also become quiet; but the silence was even more frightening. Resting on its spindly legs, the machine had the look of an insect digesting its prey. I remembered my glimpse of the derelict tractor in the night; this insect was as tall as King Kong.

For what seemed a long time, nothing happened. The thing didn't stir, and there was no sound or movement from the house. All was still; not even a bird chirped. The tentacle hovered in midair, motionless and rigid.

When, after a minute or so, the tentacle did move, it raised itself higher, as though making a salute. For a second or two it hung in the air, before slamming down violently against the roof. Slates scattered, and rafters showed through a gaping hole. The woman started to shriek again.

Methodically the tentacle smashed the house, and as methodically picked over the ruins, like a scavenger going through a garbage can. The shrieking stopped, leaving just the din of demolition. A second tentacle set to work alongside the first, and a third joined them.

They probed deep into the rubble, lifting things up to the level of the panels. Most of what was picked up was dropped or tossed aside—chairs, a sideboard, a double bed, a bathtub dangling the metal pipes from which it had been ripped. A few were taken inside: I noticed an electric kettle and a television set.

At last it was over, and dust settled as the tentacles retracted under the capsule.

"I think we ought to get away from here," Andy said. His voice was so low I could hardly hear him.

"How far do you think it can see?"

"I don't know. But if we dodge out quickly, and get round the back . . ."

I gripped his arm. Something was moving at the base of the rubble that had been the farmhouse: a black dog wriggled free and started running across the farmyard. It covered about ten meters before a tentacle arrowed towards it. The dog was lifted, howling, in front of the panels, and held there. I thought it was going to be taken inside, as the man had been; instead the tentacle flicked it away. Briefly the dog was a black blur against the dawn light, then a crumpled silent heap.

The sick feeling was back, and one of my legs was trembling. I thought of my first sight of the Eiffel Tower, the summer my mother left and Ilse came to live with us—and my panicky feeling over the way it stretched so far up into the sky. This was as if the Eiffel Tower had moved—had smashed a house to bits and swallowed up a man . . . tossed a dog to its death the way you might throw away an apple core.

Time passed more draggingly than I ever remembered. I looked at my watch, and the display read 05:56. I looked again after what seemed like half an hour, and it said 05:58. The sky was getting lighter and there was first a point of gold, then a sliver, finally a disk of sun beyond the ruins of the house. I looked at my watch again. It was 06:07.

Andy said, "Look!"

The legs hadn't moved but the capsule was tilting upwards and beginning a slow rotation. The row of panels was moving to the left. Soon we might be out of the field of vision and have a chance of sneaking away. But as the rotation continued, a second row of panels came into view. It could see all round.

When it had traversed a hundred and eighty degrees, the rotation stopped. After that, nothing happened. The monster just stayed there, fixed, as leaden minutes crawled by.

The first plane came over soon after eight. A fighter made two runs, east to west and then west to east at a lower level. The thing didn't move. A quarter of an hour later a helicopter circled round, taking photographs, probably. It was nearly midday before the armored brigade arrived. Tanks and other tracked vehicles drew up on open farmland, and, in the bit of the farm lane in view, we could see an important-looking car and some trucks, including a TV van, all keeping a careful distance.

After that, nothing happened for another long time. We learned later this was the period in which our side was attempting to make radio contact, trying different frequencies without result. Andy got impatient, and again suggested making a run for it, towards the tanks.

I said, "The fact it hasn't moved doesn't mean it won't. Remember the dog."

"I do. It might also decide to smash this hut."

"And if we run, and it starts something and the army starts something back . . . we're likely to catch it from both sides."

He reluctantly accepted that. "Why *hasn't* the army done something?"

"What do you think they ought to do?"

"Well, not just sit there."

"I suppose they don't want to rush things. . . ."

I broke off as an engine started up, followed by a rumble of tracks. We ran to the window. A single tank was moving forward. It had a pole attached to its turret, and a white flag fluttering from the pole.

8

The tank lurched across the field and stopped almost directly beneath the capsule. The engine switched off, and I heard a sparrow chirruping outside the shed. Then, unexpectedly, there was a burst of classical music.

I asked, "Where's that coming from?"

"From the tank, I think."

"But why?"

"Maybe they want to demonstrate that we're civilized, not barbarians. It's that bit from a Beethoven symphony, isn't it—the one that's sung as a European anthem?"

"That's crazy," I said.

"I don't know." Andy pointed. "Look."

The machine was showing signs of movement. Beneath the capsule a tentacle uncurled. It extended down towards the tank and began waving gently.

"What's it *doing*?" I asked.

"Maybe it's keeping time."

The weird thing was, he was right; it was moving in rhythm with the music. A second tentacle emerged, dipped, and brushed against the turret. As though it were getting the hang of things, the first tentacle started moving faster, in a more positive beat. The second felt its way round the tank from front to rear, then made a second approach from the side, moving over it and probing underneath. The tip dug down, rocking the tank slightly, and re-emerged to complete an embrace. The tank rocked more violently as it was lifted, at first just clear of the ground, then sharply upward.

9

Abruptly the music gave way to the stridence of machine-gun fire. Tracer bullets flamed against the sky. The tank rose in the tentacle's grip until it was level with the panels. It hung there, spitting out sparks.

But pointlessly; at that angle the tracers were scouring empty sky. And they stopped abruptly, as the tentacle tightened its grip; armorplate crumpled like tinfoil. For two or three seconds it squeezed the tank, before uncurling and letting it drop. The tank fell like a stone, landing on its nose and balancing for an instant before toppling over. There was a furrow along the side where it had been compressed to less than half its original width.

Andy said, "That was a Challenger." He sounded shaken, but not as shaken as I felt. I could still see that terrible careless squeeze, the tank dropped like a toffee paper.

When I looked out again, one of the tentacles had retracted, but the other was waving still, and still in the rhythm it had picked up from the music. I wanted to run—somewhere, anywhere, not caring what came next—but I couldn't move a muscle. I wondered if anyone in the tank had survived. I didn't see how they could have.

Then, unexpectedly and shatteringly, there was a roar of aircraft as the fighter-bombers, which had been on standby, whooshed in from the south, launching rockets as they came. Of the six they fired, two scored hits. I saw the long spindly legs shatter,

10

the capsule tilt and sway and crash. It landed between the ruins of the farmhouse and the wrecked
tank, with an impact that shook the shed.

I could hardly believe how quickly it was over—
and how completely. But there was the capsule lying
on its side, with broken bits of leg sticking out. As
we stared, a second wave of fighter-bombers
swooped in, pulverizing the remains.

◎ ◎ ◎
TWO

The school term started three weeks later. By then the big excitement—with Andy and me being interviewed on television and local radio and all that—was over, but people at school were still interested. They fired questions at us—mostly me, because Andy was less willing to talk. I talked too much and then regretted it. When Wild Bill brought the subject up in physics class, I no longer wanted to discuss it, least of all with him.

He didn't look wild and his name wasn't Bill; he was a small, neat gray-haired man with a clipped voice and a sarcastic manner. His name was Hockey, and he had a habit of swinging round from the board and throwing whatever was in his hand—a piece of chalk usually—at someone he thought might be misbehaving behind his back. On one occasion it was the board eraser, which was wooden and quite heavy, and he hit a boy in the back row on the fore-head. We called him Wild Bill Hockey after Wild Bill Hickock.

"Come on, Cordray," he said, "don't be shy. Now that you're famous you owe something to those of us who aren't." Some of the girls tittered. "The first person to see a Tripod, as I gather the media has decided we shall call them. . . . You'll be in the history books for that, even if not for the Nobel Prize in Physics."

There was more tittering. I'd been second from bottom the previous term.

"It throws an interesting light on national psychology," Wild Bill went on, "to consider the various reactions to man's first encounter with creatures from another part of the universe."

He had a tendency, which most of us encouraged, to launch into discourses on things that interested him, some of them quite remote from physics. I was happier still if it got him off my back.

He said, "As you know, there were three landings; one in the United States, in Montana, one in Kazakhstan in the Soviet Union, and Cordray's little show on the edge of Dartmoor. The landings were roughly simultaneous, ours in the middle of the night, the American late the previous evening and the Russian in time for breakfast.

"The Americans spotted theirs first, after tracking it in on radar, and just surrounded it and waited. The Russians located the one in their territory fairly quickly too, and promptly liquidated it with a rocket strike. We played Beethoven to ours, sent in a single tank, and then smashed it after it had destroyed the tank. Is that a testimony to British moderation? Cordray?"

I said unwillingly, "I don't know, sir. After it wrecked the farmhouse, I didn't care how soon they finished it off."

"No, I don't suppose you did. But presumably you had no more notion than the military of what a pushover it was going to be. And that, of course, is the fascinating part." He ran his fingers through his thinning hair.

"When I was your age there was a war on. We had a physics class similar to this interrupted one afternoon by a V-2 rocket that landed a quarter of a mile away and killed fifteen people. It was alarming, but I didn't really find it *interesting*. What interested me more than the war was what I read in the science-fiction magazines of those days. Rockets being hurled from Germany to England to kill people struck me as dull, compared with the possibilities of their being used to take us across interplanetary space to discover exotic life forms—or maybe bring them here to us.

"Science-fiction writers have portrayed that second possibility in a variety of ways. We have read of, or more recently watched on screen, alien invaders of every shape and size, color and texture, from overgrown bloodsucking spiders to cuddly little creatures

14

with long snouts. Their arrival has been shown as bringing both disaster and revelation. What no one anticipated was a Close Encounter of the Absurd Kind, a cosmic farce. Why do I say farce, Cordray?"

"I don't know, sir."

"Well, you saw it, didn't you? Consider the Tripods themselves, for a start. What sort of goons would dream up something so clumsy and inefficient as a means of getting around?"

Hilda Goossens, a tall, bony redhead who was the class genius and his favorite, said, "But they must have had very advanced technology. We know they couldn't have come from within our solar system, so they must have traveled light-years to get here."

Wild Bill nodded. "Agreed. But consider further. Although the Americans didn't approach their Tripod, they did try the experiment of driving animals close in. Night had fallen by that time. And the Tripod switched on ordinary white light—searchlight beams, you could say—to find out what was happening beneath its feet. So it looks as though they don't even have infrared!

"And having gone to the considerable trouble of dropping these three machines at various points of the planet, think of what they used them for. Two out of three just sat around; the third demolished a farmhouse and *then* sat around. And a single sortie from a single air force squadron was sufficient to reduce it to mechanical garbage. The other two put up no better defense; the one in America actually self-destructed without being attacked. In fact, altogether the dreaded invasion from outer space proved to be the comic show of the century."

Some laughed. Although I'd done my bit of crawling to Wild Bill in the past, I didn't join in. I could still see it too clearly—the insectlike shape towering above the ruins of the farmhouse, the snaky tentacles plucking up pathetic bits and pieces and tossing them away. . . . It hadn't been funny then, and it wasn't now.

Pa and I moved in with my grandmother after my mother left us. Grandpa had died not long before, and she was glad to have us take over part of the big house. It was a long, low granite building, and you reached her wing through a connecting door, which was mostly used from her side. She didn't like us going through to her without prior warning. She was very positive altogether about what she liked and didn't like. I had to call her Martha, for instance, not Granny. She was in her seventies, but very active; she took some keeping up with on walks.

After my father married Ilse, I think our being on tap suited her even better. Because Ilse was Swiss, she spoke several languages, which Martha found useful in her business. She had an antiques shop in Exeter and traveled around a lot, on the Continent sometimes, looking for things to buy. Ilse often went with her, and helped out generally.

Grandpa, who had been an army officer, was in

poor health for several years before he died, and one of my earliest memories was of being shushed if I made any noise around him. Martha wasn't one of those warm, cozy grannies you read about, and things didn't change after we moved into the house. She wasn't someone to chat with. When I asked her about my mother once, she headed the conversation off briskly, and went on about how lucky I was having Ilse. If she was fond of anyone it was my half sister, Angela, and, in a bossy way, of my father. There was also my Aunt Caroline, but we didn't see much of her. On the whole, I always felt Martha was more at home with antiques than people.

She and Ilse were in the sitting room when Andy and I came in from a bike ride one Saturday afternoon—we'd cut it short when it started raining. They were pricing antiques, with Angela helping. Angela was seven, blonde and pretty and quite bright, I suppose. Pa was dotty about her. She was holding a china dog and saying how beautiful it was, and Martha was smiling at her. She loved people loving china and stuff. I could never work out how much of a creep my half sister was.

I asked, "OK if I turn on the TV?"

Ilse said, "Is it all right, Martha?"

"No," Martha said crisply. "I cannot be distracted while I'm doing this. What *did* I give for the warming plate? My memory's going totally."

Ilse gave me one of her helpless placating looks that always maddened me. She wasn't going to argue with Martha, but she wanted to put things right with me some other way.

"Lowree, in the kitchen are some chocolate chip cookies I make fresh this morning. If you wish, you find them in the little stone jar. . . ."

I cut across. "No, thanks."

Actually they were one of the few things she cooked I really liked, but I wasn't in the mood for accepting bribes. I thought how much I hated the way she called me Lowree, and that accent of hers altogether. It really made me cringe when I heard her talking to teachers at school on open days.

Besides, we'd bought Mars bars at the village shop on the way back from the ride. Andy looked as though he still wouldn't mind taking chocolate chip cookies on board, so as a distraction I renewed a wrangle we'd been having earlier. He'd read something about the destruction of the Tripods being the greatest crime in history: first contact with another intelligent species, and we'd blown it. I didn't care that much, but didn't feel like agreeing, either.

I reminded him he hadn't felt so friendly towards the Tripod when we were in the hut. He said that didn't mean one couldn't look at it in a balanced way afterwards.

I said, "And don't forget the Tripod did the attacking in the first place. You saw what happened to the farmhouse."

"Our people could still have taken time to find out more about it. It was obviously on a scouting expedition. Destroying the farmhouse could have been just a mistake."

"The tank carried a white flag."

"And played classical music," Andy said, sneering. "That's bound to be a big deal for creatures from another solar system."

I was the one who'd thought it crazy at the time, but it wasn't unusual in arguments with Andy for us to switch sides. I said, "They may have got it wrong, but at least they were trying to be civilized. And the Americans didn't do anything to theirs, but it still blew itself up."

"I should think two out of three destroyed would be enough to brand this a hostile planet. They called it off, and exploded the last one so as to leave as few clues as possible to their own technology. In case we came after them, I suppose. They knew we had rockets, so we were obviously on the verge of interplanetary flight."

I was tired of the subject. Maybe we *had* passed up our one chance of establishing contact with aliens. I hadn't been worrying about it at the time, and it didn't bother me too much now.

I said, "Anyway, it's finished. They won't come again after a battering like that. Feel like a go on the computer? I've got a new Dragons game."

Andy looked at his watch. "I'd better be getting back. It's nearly five, and I told Miranda I'd be home early. She's going out."

Miranda was his mother; like Martha, she insisted

19

on Christian names. She went out a lot, which was why Andy came to our place so much. I'd heard Pa and Ilse talking once about his not having a secure home. They were very keen on secure homes. If Andy's was insecure, it didn't seem to bother him.

Angela must have been listening. "That new show's on at five," she said, and switched on the television. I watched in silence, thinking what Martha would have said if I'd done it. Martha stretched and yawned.

"I think that finishes the pricing. Quite a good batch, really. Which show is that, Angel?"

"The Trippy Show."

Behind the credits the screen was full of cartoon Tripods whirling round in a crazy dance. The program was supposed to have been inspired by the Tripod invasion. The music was wild, too—blasts of heavy metal and rock mixed up with traditional, including one quite catchy tune.

"I don't think it's going to be quite my kind of thing," Martha said.

Angela, sitting cross-legged on the carpet, paid no attention. Martha didn't say anything about switching off.

I said to Andy, "I'll cycle over with you. Nothing better to do."

My father was wiry, not very tall, and wore glasses. He looked like an athletic version of Woody Allen, but didn't talk so fast. He was a real-estate agent and spent a lot of time out, weekends included.

I couldn't recall much of the way things had been between him and my mother, except for the silences, which sometimes lasted days. And I could remember them talking separately to me, as though they were at the end of two different bowling alleys with a single set of pins, me being the pins. There was nothing like that with Ilse. He talked his head off both to her and to Angela. He never seemed to talk much to me, though. I reckoned I got about three percent of his conversation, and even that he had to work at.

One Sunday I found myself alone because he was showing a house to clients and Martha had taken the others to a mobile antiques market. She asked me if I wanted to come, and I said no, I had a load of homework. That was only partly true; I'd done most of it on Friday evening.

When I'd finished the rest, I was at a loose end. I made myself a bacon sandwich, played the Dragons game a bit, skimmed through the comic section of the Sunday paper. It was still only a quarter to eleven. I was wondering about telephoning Andy when I heard Pa's car in the drive.

He said, "Where's everybody? Oh yes, the antiques market. Feel like going along to surprise them, Laurie?"

"We wouldn't find them."

"It's at Budlake, isn't it? On the Green."

"There are a couple of other places Martha said they might go on to."

"We might still catch them there."

I didn't say anything. He looked at me with a slightly bothered expression.

"Something else you'd rather do?"

"We haven't been on the boat lately."

"It's a bit late in the year. And not the best weather."

There'd been a gale in the night. It was dying down, but the wind was gusting sharply and the sky full of gray clouds chasing each other's tails.

I said, "We could check the mooring."

He paused. "Sure, Laurie, we could do that."

We'd had the boat for two years. It was a Moody 30, with seven berths in three cabins. It had bilge keels, a Bukh 20 h.p. diesel engine, Decca navigation and Vigal radar, with a big refrigerator in the galley, and a shower. Pa had bought it, secondhand, on the strength of his firm having a good year through the boom in house prices.

Pa talked a bit on the way to the river. I didn't mind just listening. Then gradually he dried up, and we were back into the usual silence. I found myself resenting it as usual, too, then decided to do something about it.

I said, "Did you see the report about the body they found in the Tripod wreck having been dissected? Well, its head, at least. I suppose they kept that part back at first so as not to scare people."

"You could be right."

"But there was no sign of anything that could have *done* the dissecting."

"Remote-control robot, probably. Part of all that melted-down machinery they found in the capsule."

I said, "He just happened to run out of the farmhouse. If it had been Andy or me, running out of the shed, it could have been one of us that got dissected."

Pa was silent.

I said, "You've never said how you felt about it—when it was happening."

"Didn't I?"

I said sharply, "I'd have remembered if you had."

"I remember that morning," Pa said slowly. "I remember it very well. I woke early, and there was a bit on the six o'clock news about a strange object on Dartmoor. They gave more at six thirty, mentioning how big it was and the three legs, and that there was a report of something similar from America. Then at seven they dropped it completely, except to say there was a Ministry of Defense order banning traffic from certain roads. I worked out they were sealing off an area of Dartmoor. Remembering what you'd said on the telephone about orienteering, I also worked out you were probably inside it."

I felt a bit uncomfortable. "It was a big area. There were half a dozen other teams who didn't see anything."

"The point was, I was pretty sure you were somewhere around there, and it looked as though something nasty was happening. I started making calls—to the police first, then the BBC—in the end to the Ministry of Defense. They were so bland and cagey, I knew it must be serious. I lost my temper and shouted. It didn't get me anywhere."

Normally Pa was easy tempered and anxious to please with people he didn't know. The thought of him losing his temper made me feel better.

He went on, "I was on the point of getting the car out and driving there—seeing if I could force a way in. Then there was the news of the air strike, and that whatever it was had been destroyed. I thought I'd better hang on by the telephone for news of you. It was a long wait."

I said, "We were all right in the shed."

He took a hand off the wheel to squeeze my shoulder.

"You did the sensible thing, lying low. Andy said you argued him out of making a run for it. When I was talking to Ilse, she said we could rely on you being sensible."

I moved away from his hand.

He said, "You know, Laurie, Ilse's very fond of you." I didn't say anything. "As fond as she is of Angela."

Which made it silly.

I said, "I hope the boat's all right. It was wild in the night."

"Our bit of the river's sheltered except from a true southerly. The wind was well west of south."

24

We'd used the boat a lot the first season, but much less since. Ilse wasn't keen—maybe because the only boating in Switzerland was on lakes. She usually got sick. She didn't complain, or refuse to come out on the *Edelweiss*—what a name for a boat!—but trips tailed off.

"We never did make that trip to Guernsey."

I don't know if I sounded accusing. He was apologetic. He talked about the work tying him up, and his partner being away sick. And Martha had been busy, too, and we needed to fit in with her. Martha had a small property in the Channel Island of Guernsey which we used for holidays. Or had done, previous years. This year Pa and Ilse and Angela had gone to Switzerland to stay with Ilse's parents; her father (we called him the Swigramp) hadn't been well. So I went to summer camp.

"We'll make it next year definitely," Pa said. "Early maybe. Easter. How about Easter?"

"Sounds great," I said.

I was doing my homework when the telephone rang. I picked it up, thinking it might be Andy. I couldn't make out more than a word or two from the other end, but recognized the speaker as the Swigram, Ilse's mother. She had an accent that made Ilse sound like a BBC announcer.

I said, speaking slowly and deliberately, "This is Laurence. I will get her. Please hold the line. *Warten Sie, bitte.*"

I called Ilse and went to my room. I'd left the

25

radio on and they were playing the Trippy record. It was the theme music from the TV show, with a sound-synthesizer vocal added, which had gone to the top of the charts in a week. The words were stupid, the music was jangly and repetitive, and the synthetic voice was irritating, but it was the sort of number that gets under your skin and has you humming and being driven mad by it at the same time. The show had become fantastically popular all round the world, including Russia and China. I still hadn't watched it, partly because Angela was a total fan, but I could feel the music grabbing me in an insidious sort of way.

When I finished my homework, I went through to the sitting room. Ilse and Pa were there; he'd poured drinks and they were talking.

I arrived to hear Ilse saying, "Any attack is serious. And since a long time, he is not well."

"I just meant," Pa said, "you could wait and see, for a day or so."

"Then it is maybe too late."

"Something wrong with the Swigramp?" I asked.

Pa nodded. "Heart attack." He went on to Ilse, "From what you say she said, it doesn't sound desperate. He's not even in intensive care."

"But it is desperate for *her.*" She looked at Pa, in an exhausted, wounded way. "I do not wish to go. You know that. But . . ."

Her voice drifted off. He went to her and she put her arms round him. I looked out of the window. A

26

mistle thrush and a blackbird were fighting over the orange berries on the creeper that covered the side wall.

Pa said, "I'll get you on the first possible flight. What about Angel?"

"Do you think it best she comes with me?"

Very much best, I thought. At that moment I saw Angela come in to the drive and lean her bicycle against the wall. Ilse saw her, too, and called her in. She explained that *Grossvater* was ill with a heart attack, that she needed to go to Switzerland to see him and *Grossmutti,* and that she thought it might be best for Angela to go with her.

"When?" Angela asked.

"As soon as Papa will get flights. Sometime tomorrow."

"Before the Pony Club gymkhana?"

They'd got a pony for her in early summer, a little Shetland with a nasty temper, called Prince. It had bitten me twice and tried to kick me, but Angela was crazy about it. She'd been weeks practicing for the Pony Club event.

"I forget Pony Club," Ilse said.

"If you want me to come . . ."

"No, you stay. If he is all right, I am maybe not long away."

Angela hugged her mother. She was good at getting her own way without causing trouble, as I tended to.

I thought about the Swigramp. He was thickset,

and red-faced from having lived all his life more than fifteen hundred meters above sea level. He spoke good English because of running a guesthouse, but I'd never talked much with him. It was different where Angela was concerned; I had a feeling he'd be even happier to see her than Ilse. It was tough on him that she was more hooked on a pony.

People had different priorities. I was sorry about his heart attack, but not about Ilse leaving. It would have been better if Angela had been going, too, but you can't have everything.

◎ ◎ ◎
THREE

About a week after Ilse went to Switzerland, I finally caught a Trippy Show. Pa was out, and Martha had taken Angela to the shop. She'd refused to go at first because she wanted to watch, and rather than have her stick around I'd promised to videotape it for her. I switched on, and started to watch it myself.

It was a mixture of cartoon, live action, stills, and abstract, the abstract using all the old computerized design tricks and a few new ones. The cartoons were very detailed and realistic, animated paintings almost, and even the abstract bits were full of Tripod shapes. The whole thing was backed up by music which seemed chaotic but after a time built into a pattern of sounds and rhythms which weirdly hung together.

I'd heard it was a comic show, poking fun at the

Tripods as stupid giants that lumbered around and got into trouble, getting their legs tied in knots and falling over—that sort of thing. It was like that to start with, but later the attitude changed. The second part featured a maiden in distress, imprisoned and tied up by a nasty-looking dragon, and a knight trying to rescue her. It was comic-book historical, with him in shining armor and her in a long dress, with one of those hoodlike things I think they call a wimple on her head.

The knight's rescue attempts kept on going wrong in ludicrous ways. Some of them were funny, and I laughed once or twice. But gradually it became less funny than frightening: what you could see of the girl's face had a desperate look, the knight was sweating with fear, and the dragon was more sinister and had doubled in size.

The climax saw the knight pinned down beneath one of the dragon's feet, a claw through his armor and realistic blood dripping into the dust, and the dragon's jaws moving down towards the girl's head. The music was jagged and ugly, backed by a drumbeat like a death roll. There was a shot of the knight's face, and he looked as dead as I'd ever seen. It gave me the shivers.

That was when the Tripod came over the horizon, with dawn behind it and the music changing. It turned into the Trippy theme, but tricked out with extra harmonies and an orchestra which had everything from an organ to hunting horns. It sounded vigorous and hopeful. The silvery tentacles had a gentle gleam, not the hard metal glare I remem-bered, as they swished out of the sky—one to release the girl, a second to lift up the knight, the third to drive like a spear into the puffed-out chest of the drag-on.

It ended with the girl freed, the knight revived, and the pair of them mounted on his horse and rid-ing off into the dawn. The dragon dissolved first into bones, then dust. And the Tripod presided over the scene, with the rising sun throwing a halo round its capsule. There was the Trippy tune and massed voices roaring "Hail the Tripod! Hail the Tripod! Hail the Tripod!" On and on.

I'd watched it right through and it certainly hadn't been boring, but it left me without any desire to see another Trippy Show. But I knew a lot of people were crazy on it, like Angela. Though the craze wasn't confined to kids—a lot of adults were fans.

I ran the tape back, and hit the playback button to check. The beginning of an antiques program Mar-tha had videotaped came up. I thought I must have started recording partway in, but as the man droned on about some worm-eaten writing desk I realized what had happened. It was something I'd done be-fore, pressing RECORD with the set tuned to TV in-stead of VCR.

When they came back, I was in my room. I heard the car stop and the front door open, and Angela's voice yelling for me. I thought it best to get it over with. I found her in the hall.

"Where is it? The tape. You didn't label it."

"No, I missed it. I'm sorry."

"What?"

"I was watching on the TV channel, and forgot to switch to video."

"It's not funny, Laurie. Where's the tape?"

I shook my head, and she saw I meant it.

"You can't have done." Her voice rose to a howl. "You can't have, you can't! You couldn't be so rotten!"

Martha came in to find her sobbing, and asked what was the matter.

I said, "I forgot to record the Trippy Show. At least, I didn't forget . . ."

Martha said coldly, "You promised her."

"I know. And I tried to." The sobbing was getting louder and wilder; I had to raise my own voice to be heard. "Anyway, I don't think it's a program kids ought to watch. I don't think you would either, if you'd seen it. You've always gone on about violence on TV, and . . ."

Angela's face was white and tense. Without warning she came at me like a small but savage bull. I grabbed the stairpost to avoid going over, and the bull turned into a cat, clawing wildly. I heard Martha's voice, shocked, saying "Angel," and then was too busy defending myself. It was silly—she was only seven and not particularly big for her age—but I realized I needed to use all my strength to hold her off. In the end I managed to pin her against the stairs. She struggled and screamed for quite a bit; then went limp.

32

She lay slumped as I stood up.

Martha said, "What have you done to her?"

"Nothing. Only tried to stop her killing me."

I felt a trickle down my cheek and my hand came away smeared with blood. Martha was stooping beside Angela. She said, "Angel, are you all right?"

Angela didn't answer, but the sobbing started again; no longer violent, just miserable. Martha said we should get her to bed. We practically had to carry her.

Martha discussed it with Pa that evening. Angela was still in her room, and he went up to see her.

When he came down, he said, "She seems all right."

"I was worried," Martha said. "She was—well, violent."

Pa said, "Children do have storms for no reason." He smiled at me. "Laurie did, when he was that age."

I remembered a particular time, when he'd said he would play football with me and hadn't. When he finally came out, I kicked him instead of the ball, and went on kicking him. I'd had a good reason, though. That was before Ilse came to live with us, but I knew about her; and I knew he'd been talking to her on the telephone and had forgotten his promise to me.

Angela seemed normal when she came down, at least as far as the others were concerned; she didn't speak to me. Martha went to fix supper, and she headed for the stack of videotapes. We both saw what she picked out: one of the Trippy Shows.

Pa said, "I don't think we want that, Angel."

"There's time. Martha said half an hour."

"All the same . . ."

I expected her to go into one of her wheedling routines, but her face was expressionless as she stared at him, holding the cassette.

Pa said, after a moment, "Well, keep it quiet. I think I'll go to the study phone, and find out what the weather in the Alps is like."

I went to my room. The Trippy music followed me up the stairs.

We had double physics on Monday morning, which made a depressing start to the week. Wild Bill was late and we gossiped. Talk got round to the Trippy Show, and I noticed the difference in reactions, some saying it was lousy and others raving about it. There didn't seem to be any logical way of working out who was likely to be for, and who against.

Andy just said he thought it a bit silly. I said it wasn't silly, it was zilch, and poked fun at the bit with the knight and the dragon.

Rodney Chambers, in the row in front of me, said, "What do *you* know?"

I was surprised, not by the remark but by his making it. I couldn't remember him expressing an opinion about anything before. I said, "I know a load of rubbish when I see it. My little sister goes for it, though. I suppose it's her age level."

34

Chambers stood up. "Shut up," he said. "Or I'll shut you up!"

He doubled a fist. That was surprising—he never got into fights, either—but it was his expression that hit me. It was exactly like the one on Angela's face before she went into that demented attack. The others were watching. I shrugged and tried to grin it off.

"The Trippy Show is the best thing on television." He leaned forward. "Say it, Cordray!"

The classroom door opened, and Wild Bill came in.

"A little preclass discussion, ladies and gentlemen? But not of physics, I suspect." He ran his fingers through his hair as he came to stand in front of us. "Did I catch a reference to the Trippy Show? Oddly enough, I watched it myself the other day, and liked it more than I had anticipated. It has a curious, and curiously strong, appeal."

He was silent for a moment or two. "Yes, curiously strong. But I suppose we'd better consider physics. Chapter Nine, I think."

Pa didn't tell Ilse about Angela's crazy fit, I suppose so as not to worry her. He telephoned her every evening as soon as he got in. It seemed the Swigramp was no worse, but no better. She wanted to come back, but felt she had to stay because another attack might kill him.

It suited me. Martha was tougher than Ilse—no

35

bribing treats—but I knew where I was with Martha. Angela didn't seem to be missing her mother, either, but nowadays all Angela was interested in was the Trippy Show. She didn't even seem to care about her pony, and Martha had to remind her about exercising and mucking out. She had all the shows on tape—she'd got the one I'd missed from somewhere—and hogged the VCR playing them. Martha tried cutting down, but Angela went hysterical on her, and she didn't push it. She'd joined the new Trippy fan club, and got a lot of stuff through the mail.

I overheard Martha telling Pa one night they ought to do something about it.

Pa said, "Kids have these crazes."

"But not behaving the way she does when one tries to curb her. I'm not sure she doesn't need treatment."

"I thought you despised psychiatry?"

"I think Geoffrey should see her, at least."

Geoffrey Monmouth was our doctor. He and Pa played golf together.

"I don't see the need."

His voice was resentful, perhaps because he didn't like the idea of admitting there could be anything wrong with his Angel, especially to someone in the golf club.

"You haven't seen her in a mood."

Pa didn't answer.

"There are other things to be concerned about,

36

you know, apart from when Ilse might be coming back."

I'd been listening from the hall. I turned away and went up to my room.

A couple of days later, the *Daily Mail* came out against Trippies. We didn't have that paper at home but it was being passed around in the playground when I got to school. There was a banner head-line:

TRIPPY BRAINWASH?

Underneath they asked, Is THIS SHOW A MENACE TO OUR YOUNG? They went on to quote from a couple of psychologists, saying the Trippy cult could be dangerous because it was developing a fanatical following which showed signs of getting out of hand. They gave examples of children behaving in ways which made Angela's craziness seem dead normal. One boy had tried to burn the house down when his Trippy tapes were taken from him; and a girl of thir-teen had almost killed her father with a kitchen knife. They claimed things were even worse in other countries: in the United States and Germany, kids were leaving home in droves to live together in Trippy communes. As fast as they were brought back, they took off again.

One of the Trippy fans at school produced a lighter, and set fire to the newspaper in the play-ground. The rest watched it flare up; their faces were like some I saw in a movie about people burning witches.

They were still muttering at the beginning of first class, which happened to be physics. The noise didn't stop when Wild Bill came in, and I expected him to erupt. He was tight on classroom discipline. Instead he looked at the Trippy fans in a funny way, fondly almost.

He said, "I saw you burn that evil newspaper. They had one in the common room, and I burned it, too."

The Trippy fans were still cheering him when the school secretary, Mr. Denlum, knocked and entered. He was a little man and timid, especially where Wild Bill was concerned. He went close and whispered something. Wild Bill smiled contemptuously.

"If the headmaster wishes to see me, I am of course at his disposal."

He told us to get on with our work and went out, with Denlum creeping after him. At the door he stopped and turned round, still smiling. He cried out, shouted almost, "Hail the Tripod!"

Trippies were the lead in the television news that evening. They showed a mob of them rioting outside the *Daily Mail* offices, and scuffles when police tried to disperse them. There were Trippies being dragged into police vans, a policeman with blood running down his face. The announcer said that another mob had assembled outside the editor's home.

Windows had been smashed and Tripod figures daubed on the walls.

"In the House of Commons this afternoon," he went on, "the prime minister said that the situation is being closely watched. There is particular concern that the practice of Trippy cultists banding together to live communally has now spread to this country. It is reported that there are several groups in London, squatting in empty flats and offices, and that similar communes have been set up in a number of provincial cities, including Birmingham and Exeter."

Martha said, "I can't think why they've let things get this far. It needs tackling with a firm hand."

"Easier said than done," Pa said.

"That's the whole trouble. Too much saying, too little doing."

The news reader started talking about stocks and shares and a financial panic, and Angela, who had been sitting staring at the screen, got up and left the room. Martha and Pa went on talking about the rioting. She was getting angrier, and he was agreeing; he never liked being on the wrong side of her for long. He was saying yes, the Trippy Show should be banned, when I heard the front door open and close.

I said, "That was Angela."

Pa turned to me. "What?"

"Just then. Going out."

He asked Martha, "Did she say anything to you?"

"No. I suppose she could have gone to Emma's."

Emma was a friend of hers in the village.

I said, "There was that bit on the news, about a Trippy commune in Exeter."

"She couldn't—" Martha began. Pa went for the front door, and I followed him. Emma's house was a couple of hundred yards to the left. Angela was heading right, in the direction of the bus station.

Pa needed my help in bringing her back; she fought for some time before suddenly going slack on us. He carried her to her room, and Martha and I watched her. She lay staring at the ceiling. When Pa came back she didn't answer his questions, didn't look at him or even move. Dr. Monmouth turned up a few minutes later. He lived close by.

He was a small man, shorter than Pa, with a pink and white baby face and wispy hair. He spoke fast, stammering a bit. Pa explained what had happened.

When he'd examined Angela and shone a light in her eyes, he said to Pa, "As you know, I use hypnosis sometimes. As we both know, it's not a line you care for. If you like, I'll sedate her and refer her to a p-pediatrician. But I would like to try hypnosis. It might just give us an idea what's troubling her. M-may I?"

Pa said reluctantly, "I don't suppose it can do any harm."

"I'm sure it can't."

Dr. Monmouth got her to sit up, handling her gently but firmly. From his bag he produced a steel ball on a chain and began to swing it in front of her.

40

I'd seen something similar on a show, but it was interesting to watch, and listen to his voice, gentle and monotonous: "You are feeling sleepy . . . sleepy . . . sleepy. . . . Your eyelids are getting heavy. . . . Your eyes are closing . . . closing. . . . You are asleep. . . ."

I was getting drowsy myself.

Dr. Monmouth slipped the ball in his pocket. He said, "Angela. Can you hear me?"

In a thick voice she said, "Yes."

"Is there anything you have to do—you *m-must* do?"

No reply.

He said, "Tell me. What is it you have to do?"

She said slowly, "Obey the Tripod."

"What does that m-mean, Angela?"

"The Tripod is good. The Tripod knows best."

"Best about what?"

"About everything."

"So what do you do?"

"I do what the Tripod tells me."

"And who told you this?"

"The Tripod."

"Did the T-Tripod tell you to run away from home and join the Trippies?"

"Yes."

Dr. Monmouth held her wrists in his hands. "Listen, Angela. Listen carefully. There is no Tripod. You have never watched the T-Trippy Show. There is no T-Trippy Show. You don't like watching televi-

41

sion. You are your own person, and no one, nothing, can rule your mind. Now, I am going to count to five, and on the count of five you will wake up, not r-remembering the words I've said, but r-remembering what I've told you. One, two, three . . ."

Her eyes opened on five. She said, "What is it?" She looked at us standing round the bed. "I've not been ill or anything?"

He smiled reassuringly. "Just a turn. You're all right now. Fit for anything. Want to watch t-television?"

"No." She shook her head violently. "No, I don't."

Angela stayed in her room, rearranging her dolls. She had more than a dozen, and I realized it was weeks since she'd played with them. I went down with the others, and Pa poured them drinks.

"I'm still not sure I know what that was about." He handed a glass to Dr. Monmouth. "She'd been previously hypnotized by someone else? But who?"

"You heard her: the Tripod."

Martha said, "That's ridiculous. The Tripods were destroyed. By the television show, do you mean? Is that possible?"

Dr. Monmouth took his drink. "Hypnosis is a state of artificially induced sleep or trance, in which the subject is susceptible to suggestion. There are various m-methods of inducing it. I've never known of it being done through television, but I wouldn't rule out the possibility."

42

"But the actual suggestion," Pa said, "how would that work?"

"It could be subliminal: a message flashed on-screen for a microsecond. Reinforced by the spoken message, 'Hail the T-Tripod.' It's interesting that it affects some people and not others. But so do other things, of course. Strobe lighting doesn't bother m-most people, but induces epilepsy in a m-minority. It could be the result of a minor cortical irregularity. A difference in alpha rhythm, perhaps, which makes them susceptible."

"But done by whom," Martha demanded, "the Russians?"

"I suppose that's possible. But the show originated in the United States."

"Why would the Americans want to do such a thing? It makes no sense."

"There have been experiments in the past with subliminal suggestion in advertising. M-maybe somebody's preparing the launch of a T-Tripod toy, and the p-project got out of hand. Or maybe it's like the mass hysteria you get with pop stars—hysteria and hypnosis both involve surrender of the will—and by some freak it's got tied in with this particular show."

Pa asked, "Which do you think?"

"I don't know. There's a third possibility."

"What?"

"Television signals aren't stopped by the ionosphere. The show originates in America, but the suggestions could be superimposed from somewhere else." He paused. "F-from space."

43

Martha shook her head. "Now that really is ridiculous."

Pa said, "From whatever was behind the Tripods, you mean? It's a bit unlikely, isn't it? The Tripods were a joke."

"Scientific knowledge doesn't have to follow the pattern we're familiar with. The Incas had a superb road system, but didn't m-manage to invent the wheel. The fact of using something as clumsy as a T-Tripod doesn't mean they might not be a long way ahead of us in studies of the m-mind, and mental processes."

Pa shook his head. "An advertising gimmick getting out of hand sounds more likely."

The television news was full of Trippies, demonstrating and chanting about the Tripod and clashing with the police. And not just in England; there were similar scenes from America and Canada, Australia and Europe. There were rumors it was happening behind the Iron Curtain, too, but we weren't shown any of that.

The media had invented the name Trippy, and they called the demonstrations Tripping. The Trippies took it up themselves, and started singing a new song to one of the minor tunes on the Trippy Show.

"Trip, trip, trip with the Tripod . . ."

Then suddenly the Trippies were on the move. It began in London. We watched the report on early evening television, and it was like a mass migration.

44

They had managed to pick up cars and vans from all over the city and were moving out into the country. Others waited by the roadside. The weather was terrible, with rain slashing out of a black sky and a near-gale blowing. They stood patiently in the rain, wet, bedraggled, uncomplaining. Many of them carried hand-lettered signs and banners: HAIL THE TRIPOD! THE TRIPOD LIVES! or just a drawing of a Tripod. Cars and vans driven by other Trippies stopped to pick them up, and crawled on, overloaded. The police watched but didn't try to do anything.

I thought about it when I went to bed. I didn't know whether or not to feel sorry for them. It had looked a miserable scene, but they hadn't seemed miserable. I wondered what it was about. Could Dr. Monmouth be right about hypnosis through signals from space? But what *for*? Why a mass exodus like that? I remembered that lemmings went in for mass migrations. They wound up in the sea.

Presumably Angela could have been among them if Dr. Monmouth hadn't broken the spell. Some of the Trippies had looked no older than she was. The thought was chilling.

In the morning I woke early. I switched on breakfast television and stared at the screen in disbelief. A Tripod stood center screen, with sodden, gray-green fields behind it. Small dots swarmed like bees about the gigantic feet.

The newscaster was talking in a breathless, unsteady voice.

"The second Tripod invasion is amazing enough in itself—and there are landings reported in Germany and the States—but this—how would you describe it?—parade of welcome? This really is incredible. . . ."

The camera zoomed into close-up. The swarm of dots turned into people. Hundreds . . . thousands of them, waving and cheering and brandishing Trippy signs.

◎ ◎ ◎
FOUR

For a time there was a stalemate. The Tripods didn't move and no one moved against them. There was no way of attacking them without killing the Trippies clustered round. The nearest Tripod to us was north of Exeter, and there were three others in England, one in Scotland between Edinburgh and Glasgow, and one in Ireland, south of Dublin. It was the same throughout the industrialized world. Someone worked out there was a Tripod for about every ten million people, mostly planted close to major centers of population.

The Trippy Show was taken off the air, but came back, and the new broadcasts were traced to high-orbit satellites. The government tried jamming, but they switched frequency—and went on switching as fast as the jammer could chase them round.

Martha said they should stop television.

Pa said, "They can't."

"Why not? They did during the war."

I wanted to ask which war—the Boer or the Crimean? It was amazing how old people could talk about The War, as though that meant something.

Pa said, "It wasn't the major channel of communication then; that was radio. You have to remember that even when I was little, less than one house in a hundred, probably, had a TV set. If they stopped it now, there'd be panic."

"They'll have to do *something.* Mrs. Golightly says her maid's Tripped. Yesterday she was rambling on about the Tripod, and this morning she didn't turn up for work."

"If nothing worse happens to us than losing the daily help, we'll not be doing badly."

I'd just come in from school. I said, "I meant to tell you—Andy's mother's gone."

Martha demanded, "Are you sure?"

"The house was empty when he got home yesterday. He thought she might be visiting, but she didn't come back. And didn't leave a note as she usually does when she goes off."

Martha looked shocked. "Do you mean he's in the house on his own?"

"I suppose so. He can look after himself."

She turned to Pa. "Go and get him. He'd better stay with us while this is on."

"I was going to ring Ilse."

She looked at him in exasperation. "That can wait."

I knew Pa was comfortably off, though he spent a lot of time moaning about money and tax bills; and I supposed Martha was fairly rich. But my Uncle Ian was a real tycoon. He ran several companies in London—all sorts of things from coffee to property development—and they had a Rolls, and a Porsche, and one of those fantastic little MR-2 sports cars for the shopping. He and Aunt Caroline (Pa's sister) spent a lot of time jetting around. He was tied in with a company in Tokyo and another in New York, and in between they lived in a real mansion in the Cotswolds, with indoor and outdoor swimming pools, tennis courts, half a dozen stables, and grounds that stretched for miles.

They had two children: Verity, who was seventeen, and Nathanael, a year older than me. (They really did call him Nathanael, even sitting round the swimming pool.) He looked like his father, with a thin, pale face and gingery hair and a weedy, slouching body, though without the potbelly Uncle Ian had got from living rich around the world. Verity was redheaded, too, but pretty.

We didn't see much of them, for a number of reasons. One was they made Ilse feel uncomfortable; another was that Martha disapproved of the way they lived. A third was *because* of the way they lived. You had to feel like a poor relation because you were. This didn't worry me too much. I envied Nathanael some of the things he took for granted (like the swimming pools), but I wouldn't have wanted them if it meant being like Nathanael, and I managed to convince myself the two went together. I might have liked Verity if she'd ever paid me any attention, but she didn't.

Pa had telephoned Aunt Caroline after what happened with Angela, partly as a warning. From what he said to Martha, I gathered she'd not been very interested; Nathanael and Verity were safe at their expensive boarding schools (Eton in Nathanael's case), and she and Ian didn't watch television. She said the Tripod business was a nuisance, all the same. They'd been planning a trip to Los Angeles—Ian was setting up a company there—but he'd decided it was best to wait till things sorted themselves out.

It was a very different Aunt Caroline who telephoned while Pa was fetching Andy. At first I couldn't make out what she was saying, her voice was so choked. It gradually emerged that though television had been banned at Eton since the second Tripod invasion, someone had been operating a set illicitly. A master had found it tuned to the Trippy Show and confiscated it, but a dozen boys had run away during the night. Nathanael was one of them.

Ian had set off at once to look for him. The nearest Tripod was on Farnham Common, not far from Eton, and they thought that was where they'd be heading. She was worried about Ian too, now.

She was still on the telephone when Pa came back with Andy. He listened to her and made big brother noises. I heard him say, "Ian will be all right, Caro.

50

I'm sure of it. And Nathanael. It's not as if they're in physical danger. It's been a week now, and nothing terrible's happened. It's just a silly business which will blow itself out. Have a drink, and try to relax. All right, have *another* drink. There are times when getting drunk's not a bad idea."

He didn't look so cheerful when he came away from the telephone. "I don't know what's going on," he said. "They called the police as soon as they heard from school, and the police didn't even pretend to help—told Ian they'd given up handling missing persons calls. There were too many of them."

Andy nodded. "That's what they told me. And some police are Tripping. The policeman at Little Ittery's gone."

That was a village five miles away. Pa said, "Try not to worry about your mother. As I told my sister, it's not as though anything terrible's happening. Nobody's been hurt. And hypnotic effects don't last. They had a doctor on the radio this morning saying he expected people to start trickling back home any time now."

I asked, "What about Angela?"

"What about her?"

"Dr. Monmouth hypnotized her. Might that not last?"

"That's different. He hypnotized her to dehypnotize her. If we find her glued to the tube again there might be reason to worry, but I've seen no sign of that."

Nor had I. I'd noticed that if anyone left the TV switched on—as Martha sometimes did when she was going out, to deter burglars—Angela switched it off.

I wasn't all that delighted about Andy staying with us. I liked him well enough, but the thought of having him twenty-four hours a day, sharing a room, didn't make me jump for joy.

That evening he got to bed first and was reading a book. That suited me, but when I got back from the bathroom, he put the book down.

"It's raining," he said. "And blowing up a storm. I wonder where Miranda is."

Even though I called Ilse by her name, it seemed wrong, his saying Miranda. After all, she was his real mother, not his stepmother. I'd never been able to work out how he really felt about her. He could talk about her weird ideas—like painting all the ceilings black—in a faintly amused way, as though she were a character in a play. At the same time, when she wasn't storming at him, he was affectionate in a way I couldn't be to anyone, let alone Ilse. He was always hugging her.

I said lamely, "She'll be all right."

"It's funny." He lay looking at the ceiling. "When she's gone off somewhere before, there've been times I hoped she wouldn't come back."

He spoke in his usual calm way. This time I didn't know what to say, and didn't try.

After a while he went on, "Of course, she'd gone those times because she wanted to. I didn't have to worry, because she was doing her own thing. I don't feel she is now." He paused. "I've been wondering if I ought to go and look for her, like your uncle with Nathanael."

I said, "You'd never find her, and if you did, what good would it do? Angela was little enough to be dragged back, and we had Dr. Monmouth round the corner. What could you do against a mob of Trippies?"

He nodded. "Not much, I suppose. But she's part of it at this moment. It's happening to her. All the mad things she did . . . And now . . . can she do anything except wave a banner and hail the Tripod?"

"It doesn't mean she's unhappy. Angela wasn't." I wouldn't have called it happy, either, but I didn't say that.

Andy looked at me. "What if it were Ilse?"

I thought about it and was aware of different feelings which I couldn't sort out. I could imagine how Pa would feel, though.

I shook my head. "I don't know."

Andy said, "I don't know, either. I just wish I could work out what it's supposed to be *for.* We know now that it's definitely linked with the Tripods, and that the people who thought up the TV show were among the first Trippies. Whatever sent the Tripods obviously monitored our television, worked out which was the most effective production center, and somehow beamed hypnotic directives into it. But what's their motivation?"

"One theory is that they come from a swamp

planet," I said, "because the only sensible reason for Tripods would be to cross marshland."

"So what sort of creature are they—intelligent giant frogs, or newts? Pigs, maybe; the pig's a swamp animal. No one knows. Maybe no one ever will. And no one has the faintest idea how their minds work. We saw what the first Tripod did to the farmhouse. This second lot seem to be doing nothing except hypnotizing people into liking them. Could that be it? They just want to be liked?"

"They're not winning as far as I'm concerned. Anyway, Pa's right. Hypnosis doesn't last. They'll start drifting back soon."

I punched my pillow and settled down. Andy was silent, and I wondered if he was still brooding about Miranda. I started thinking about Ilse and his question about how I'd feel if it had been her. But I didn't like the thoughts that came into my head, so I shut them out.

Next day was Saturday. Pa was off selling another house. People had to live somewhere, he said, Tripods or no Tripods. Martha had driven in to the shop and taken Angela. And Andy had cycled home to pick up clothes he'd forgotten the previous day.

I wandered down the garden, which had fruit trees at the bottom. Most of the apples had been picked, but there was one old tree which still had a few. Sitting on a branch and eating an apple, I thought about Ilse again. Pa had been on the tele-

54

phone to her before breakfast, urging her to come back. Afterwards he said the Swiss couldn't believe what was happening in the rest of the world. Apparently there were no Tripods in their country, and almost no Tripping.

He and Andy got into an argument about national characteristics. It wasn't the sort of thing that interested me, and I didn't pay too much attention. What I did notice was the way Pa talked to him—naturally, not going into silences and then talking too fast to make up for it. I'd left them talking. I wondered how it was he seemed able to talk easily to everyone but me.

As I tossed the apple core away, I heard a car draw up outside the house. My first thought was Pa, but the engine note was too deep for the Renault. Not Martha's Jaguar, either. I dropped out of the tree and headed back. Uncle Ian's Rolls was in the drive, and he and Nathanael beside it. Uncle Ian was wearing casual-expensive gear, blue slacks and silk roll-neck shirt, soft Gucci shoes, and a big hat. I didn't think they went with the black executive briefcase he was carrying. Nathanael had a hat, too, a woolly thing. Uncle Ian waved at me, smiling.

"I was beginning to think everyone was out."

I led the way in, explaining about the others. Surreptitiously I glanced at Nathanael. He seemed all right. Knowing Uncle Ian, he would have called someone in from Harley Street to dehypnotize him. But how had he got him back? Probably by hiring a bunch of heavies. Martha said he mixed with some funny people.

What was more puzzling was their being here, a hundred miles south of Ardaker Manor. I would have expected them to go home first. I took them into the sitting room and told Uncle Ian to pour himself a drink, as Pa would have done, and asked politely what had brought them.

He was still smiling. "There was someone I had to see, in Taunton. It's not much of a detour, so I thought I'd drop in on you."

"What about Aunt Caroline?"

He looked surprised. "What about her?"

"She was—well, worried." I glanced at my cousin, who was smiling too—unusual for him. And neither had taken his hat off. "About Nathanael."

"Oh, that. I rang her. She knows everything's all right."

I was still puzzled. Although the whiskey decanter was staring him in the face, he hadn't even looked at it. He was a pretty heavy drinker and I would have expected him to pour himself a big one, after a long drive. He walked over and put a hand on my arm.

"What you have to realize, Laurie, is that everything really *is* all right, in the biggest possible way. I'm glad we found you on your own. It makes explanations easier."

Alarm bells started to go off when he touched me. In the past I wasn't sure he'd even noticed I was there. His manner, I realized, was altogether too affable, almost ingratiating. Nothing like the way the Ardakers normally treated their poor relations.

I said, "Probably better to wait till Pa gets back. You can explain it to him, too."

He paid no attention. "A new world is dawning, you know. A world of peace and happiness."

It was all wrong. The only kind of peace and happiness he'd ever been interested in was the peace and happiness of making another fortune. I had a quick look in the direction of the door and saw, with a sinking feeling, that Nathanael was standing between it and me.

Uncle Ian went on, "It's something you have to experience to understand, but once you have, everything else is like a bad dream. For thousands of years men have fought one another, killing and torturing and enslaving. That's all gone. The Tripods are bringing peace and freedom."

"Hail the Tripod," Nathanael said.

I said, "That's very interesting."

I was wondering where the real threat lay. It was clear that far from Nathanael having been dehypnotized, his father had Tripped, too. But if all that meant was a lecture on the goodness of the Tripods, I could put up with it. I had a feeling, though, that something more serious was in view: They were looking for converts. The question was how they proposed to go about the converting. I doubted if it would just be talk. By sitting me down in front of a TV screen and forcing me to watch a Trippy Show?

But I'd watched it before and hadn't Tripped. Or by hypnotizing me some other way? Dr. Monmouth had said no one could be hypnotized against their will. If I was determined to resist, I could. Couldn't I?

"It's easy to enter the way of peace," Uncle Ian said.

His briefcase was on the carpet beside him. He clicked it open, and produced something: a floppy helmetlike thing, black, but threaded with silver.

"The lucky ones," Uncle Ian said, "are those who opened their hearts voluntarily to the Tripods' message. But the Tripods want everyone to know the joy of belonging to the new brotherhood of man. So they've given us these Caps, which will banish all doubts and uncertainties."

He held it out to me, and with his other hand pulled off his hat. He was wearing a helmet underneath.

He said earnestly, "Put it on, Laurie. Then you will know the secret of happiness, as we do."

I looked from one to the other. Neither showed hostility. Nathanael's thin features had lost their familiar sneering look and radiated goodwill. It was a chilling sight. The helmet looked harmless, just a piece of rubber with metal threads. But I felt my heart pounding.

"Sounds great," I said. "Only—can it wait a couple of minutes? I lit the gas to make coffee just before you arrived. I'd better switch off before it sets fire to the kitchen."

58

For a moment no one spoke. I started to walk towards the door, as naturally as I could.

In a calm voice, Uncle Ian said, "The human mind is full of trickery and deceit, until it has been brought into the harmony of the Tripods. Hold him, Nathanael."

I tried to push past, and, when he grabbed at me, reversed and pulled back. I ran instead for the window, which was partly open. As I did I heard a car, and saw the Jaguar stopping. I tried to clamber out, but Nathanael had my leg. I kicked and yelled for help at the same time.

My kick dislodged Nathanael and overturned the sofa. It was a barrier between them and me, but a poor and temporary one. I heard Martha outside shouting to Angela as Uncle Ian, dangling the helmet from his hand, joined Nathanael. Going for the window meant turning my back on them. I didn't know what to do and, out of panic, did nothing.

Uncle Ian said quietly, "This is silly, Laurie. No one's going to hurt you. We have something to give, and when you have it too, you'll know it's the most wonderful thing in the world. All you have to do is relax and accept."

I said, stalling for time, "Tell me more about it—about the Tripods."

He shook his head. "Trickery and deceit again. But it will soon be ended."

I'd left it too late for the window. They'd have the helmet on my head while I was struggling through.

On the window ledge was a bronze statuette of a Roman god, one of Martha's antiques. I grabbed it and held it like a club.

Uncle Ian said, "Nathanael . . ."

Nathanael leapt faster than I would have thought possible, his hand grabbing for my wrist. The speed of it and the shock made me let go of the bronze, and his hand had my wrist in a bone-twisting grip. His father was coming up behind. Looking between them I saw the door opening, and Martha.

She said, "Ian! I don't know what this is about, but let him go. At once."

He looked at her mildly. "We will bring you peace, too, Martha. After Laurie."

My grandmother was a tough old lady, but no possible match for them. She was carrying her big red crocodile handbag, the one in which she kept her stock money. I wondered if she was thinking of hitting Uncle Ian over the head with it.

I called urgently, "Get away! Get help!"

She dropped the bag with a clatter. She was holding something: black, flat-sided—a small pistol. She said, "I told you: let go of him."

Uncle Ian's voice was untroubled. "Don't be silly, Martha. We come in peace and bringing peace. No one is going to get hurt."

"That's where you're wrong." She spoke in her best bossy voice. "Unless you leave him, and get out, someone is. Badly hurt, killed perhaps."

Uncle Ian stared at her. Tripping, as we'd found

with Angela, made people almost indifferent to pain and danger. Would he call her bluff?

He shook his head slowly. "You're making such a mistake, Martha. If you'd only let me—"

He broke off as the gun exploded, shatteringly loud.

He sighed, and shrugged, and headed for the door, Nathanael following. Martha and I stood looking at each other, till we heard the Rolls start. She put out a hand, feeling for the nearest armchair, and dropped into it heavily.

"Pour me a brandy, Laurie," she said. "A stiff one."

Angela had been hiding in the shrubbery. She was more interested than frightened and wanted to see the gun, but Martha dropped it back in her bag.

I said, "I didn't know you had one."

"I got it last year, after a dealer got robbed on his way back from an antiques fair. The silly thing is, I never got 'round to practicing with it." She took the glass and gulped down brandy. "I was terrified of hitting something."

By "something" she meant one of her bits of china; her gaze ranged round the room for reassurance. The only sign of damage was a neat hole in the plaster of the wall. But she saw the bronze on the floor, and got up to examine it. The briefcase was still on the carpet where Uncle Ian had left it. I looked inside and saw more helmets.

"I wonder why he left this," I said.

Martha ran her fingers over the statuette, and said absently, "No idea."

"Except maybe he thought if he left them we'd try the helmets on, and . . . bingo!"

She shivered with repulsion. "As if we would!"

"Who can tell how a Trippy's mind works? He really thinks these things are passports to paradise, so he might think we'd be tempted. He did take the one he was trying to make me wear. Where were they heading, do you suppose? Home?"

She slammed the statuette down.

"Caroline . . ."

"What?"

She went to the telephone and dialed the number. I heard her telling Aunt Caroline what had happened. Then she said, "Caroline, listen—you must listen. . . . Leave the house before they get back. Come here. They aren't the same people, I tell you, they're dangerous. . . ."

She took the telephone from her ear and looked at it for a moment before putting it back on its rest.

I asked, "What did she say?"

I'd never seen her look helpless before.

She said, "She won't believe me. All she was concerned about was that they were alive and well. She hung up on me."

62

◎ ◎ ◎
FIVE

More went missing from school. You couldn't be sure if they were Tripping or just staying away because things were in a mess. Very little work got done, anyway.

In assembly the Head Man gave us a warning about people who might try to Cap us. It seemed Uncle Ian wasn't the only one around carrying rubber helmets. We were to report anyone acting suspiciously.

I was standing next to Hilda Goossens, who sniffed and said, "Silly old twit!"

"Why?"

"As if we need to be told."

"Someone said they saw Wild Bill hanging about school this morning. If he spots you, he might decide to Cap his pet genius."

"I *don't* think so."

"My uncle nearly managed it, with me."

She just looked at me pityingly. I wondered what it must be like to be Hilda Goossens and so sure of yourself about everything. The Head Man droned on. He was thin and anxious, white-faced and white-haired (what there was of it), due for retirement at the end of the school year. I wondered about being like him, too—just about able to cope under normal conditions, without things like Tripping to contend with.

What I was suddenly aware of was the importance of their being whatever each of them was—cocky and contemptuous, or bothered and beaten—as long as it was something they'd come to in their own way: the importance of being human, in fact. The peace and harmony Uncle Ian and the others claimed to be handing out in fact was death, because without being yourself, an individual, you weren't really alive.

The first class was meant to be chemistry, but there was no sign of the chemistry teacher. Hilda Goossens and a couple of others got on with their assignments. The rest of us talked. We stopped when the door flew open. It wasn't Mrs. Green, though, but a hairy little Welshman called Wyllie, who taught physical exercise.

He shouted, "Right! School dismissed. Everybody out."

Andy asked, "Why?"

He said importantly, "Police warning. The Exeter Tripod's on the move. The path they've plotted takes

64

it a couple of miles north, but they want everyone out of the area as a precaution. Get cracking."

A boy called Marriott said, "I live in Todpole."

Todpole was six miles north of the school. Wyllie said, "Well, you can't go there. They're evacuating along the route. It will probably be OK in an hour or two, but check with the police."

In the bike shed I waited while Andy fiddled about. The shed was empty before he straightened up. I said, "Come on—we're last."

"I've been thinking."

I said impatiently, "You can bike and think at the same time, can't you?"

"I wouldn't mind having a look at it."

It took me a moment to realize he was talking about the Tripod.

"There'll be a roadblock."

"We can get round it."

Can, not *could.* And *we,* which meant there was no way of backing out without looking chicken.

I said, "I don't suppose it's any different from the one we saw."

"No, I don't suppose it is." He wheeled his bike out of the shed. "I'd still like to take a look."

It was a bright day but the wind, blowing a swirl of leaves from the side of the road, had a wintry edge. There weren't many people about, and they were all going the opposite way.

We found the roadblock half a mile out of town.

65

A patrol car was slewed across the road with a policeman standing beside it smoking a cigarette, and another at the wheel. It was fairly obvious which way we'd need to go to get past it. To the left the ground fell away in open fields, but the higher ground on the right was wooded.

I said, "What about the bikes?"

"No sweat. Stick them in the ditch."

Mine was new from my birthday a month earlier, a racer I'd been wanting a long time. I laid it down carefully by the roadside. We got through a gap in the hedge and made for the trees. Once under cover we stayed close to the edge of the wood. We passed within a hundred yards of the patrol car. The policeman who was smoking glanced our way but gave no sign of seeing us.

If we were invisible to him, the same would presumably apply to the Tripod, which made me feel better. I even began to feel lighthearted. There were bird sounds—a blackbird, the rowdy clatter of a pheasant. Normal country stuff. This was probably a wild goose chase, anyway—a wild Tripod chase. Even if it had moved it might stop again, as the one on the moor had, or change course. The trees ended, and we ducked under a fence into a field where Friesian cows were grazing. Here high ground on our left gradually fell away, giving a view across open country. You could see for miles—fields, copses, farmhouses. In the distance, sunlight dazzled from a river.

But there was something else in the distance, too, catching the sun with a colder gleam. And moving our way; I heard the thump of its passage above the noises of birds and cows.

Andy said, "The hedge." We ran thirty meters across open meadow, and dived under. I wondered if it had seen us; it was still far off, but we didn't know its range of vision. I hoped we were hidden now. Andy squirmed forward to a position where he could look out, and after a moment's hesitation I wriggled after him, scratching my wrist on a bramble.

He whispered, "I'd forgotten how comic it looks—like a mechanical clown."

The three legs, swinging in succession, produced a motion which was a cross between lumbering and mincing. It did look ridiculous. And even though each stride covered ten or more meters, its progress seemed slow and laborious. The thumping rhythm was louder, and I caught the buzz of a helicopter, presumably shadowing it. I thought of the grace and speed of a Harrier fighter plane, and couldn't understand why this ugly thing was being allowed to bestride the land—why no one had ordered a strike the moment it moved away from its Trippies. Then, as it got closer, I could see the small specks clinging to the gigantic feet. It had brought its disciples with it. And I could hear them, singing and shouting, the words indistinguishable but the voices wild and cheerful.

"How are they managing to hang on?" Andy asked.

"I don't know." A foot slammed down, another lifted and soared across the sky, and my stomach lurched with vertigo. "I think it'll miss us by quite a bit."

I was relieved, though, when Andy nodded agreement. "By a hundred meters, I'd say. But keep your head down."

I didn't need telling. We watched the Tripod hammer its way across the valley between us and Todpole. A foot landed in water which jetted up, sparkling like diamonds. The Trippies burst into what sounded like a hymn. Then, as the next foot reached its high point, something detached and fell. The singing didn't even check as a figure dropped to earth in the next field, like a stone.

We waited till the Tripod was out of sight before going to see. It was a girl about sixteen, wearing jeans, her legs horribly jumbled. I thought she was dead as Andy bent over her. But she wasn't quite. She whispered "Hail the Tripod." Her lips barely moved, but she was smiling. The smile faded, and she really was dead.

The Tripod furthest from London had moved first, the others setting off in turn in what appeared to be a concerted march on the capital. The one on Farnham Common was the last to go, and that was when the air force was let loose. They didn't show anything on the news, but it was announced that all Tripods in Britain had been destroyed. They added that similar action had now been taken in other countries. The crisis was over. The world was finally free of Tripods.

I guessed why, although the attack on the first Tripod had been televised, these weren't. It had been a desperate decision to make. Many of the Trippies clinging to them must have been killed, and they wouldn't want to show that. It was awful thinking about it, especially since some of them could have been people I'd known. There had been no news of Andy's mother, for instance. The fact that they probably died happy, like the girl in the field, didn't make it any less terrible.

Over the next few days things were claimed to be returning to normal. It was odd, though, that so little was being said, when one remembered the fuss after the first invasion. I supposed it was to do with censorship. But why was the censorship still necessary?

Wild rumors started. One was that the royal family had Tripped and barricaded themselves inside Windsor Castle, where they were building a landing pad for the third wave of Tripods. Another said the third wave had already arrived and taken over an entire country, France in one version, the United States in another. As Pa said, censorship encouraged people to believe nonsense.

But, apart from the rumors, strange things *were* happening. People were still disappearing. In Boulder, the nearest market town, more than a hundred went at a single go. Everyone, it turned out, who had been to the Chinese take-out that evening. The following day, the county library van called at our local branch, and left taking two staff members and five people who'd just been in changing their library books. And two days after that, Todpole was declared Tripod territory. There was a big HAIL THE TRIPOD sign on the approach road, and no one was allowed in without a Cap. Caps were handed out at the roadside.

That evening Pa brought out the briefcase Uncle Ian had left. He said, "The Tripods gave them to the Trippies, and the Trippies distributed them. I don't know how many of these things there were originally, but I think there may be a lot more now."

Andy asked, "How? With all the Tripods knocked out."

Pa held up a helmet. "Simple molding and wiring, a few transistors—something that could be made by Trippies in a back room. Maybe in hundreds of back rooms, all over the world."

"Get rid of it," Martha said with loathing.

He looked at it speculatively. "I don't know."

Martha said, "I do! I want it out."

I asked, "How do you think they work?"

Pa shook his head. "No one's ever been sure how ordinary hypnosis works. But since it's a state in which people are controlled by suggestion, this could be something that induces trance—through radio waves acting directly on the electrical centers of the brain, perhaps—coupled with the command to obey the Tripods. And that command wouldn't just apply to a minority, like the one carried by TV, but to anyone wearing a helmet."

He turned it over, examining it.

"The wiring looks like a circuit. It could be linked to a control station in a satellite, or the Tripods' mother ship. In which case, breaking the circuit might put it out of action."

"Just get it out of the house," Martha said.

"But how do you get them off the Trippies' heads to do that? Oh, well." He dropped the helmet back in the briefcase. "I'll shove this in the shed for now."

I picked up the telephone the next time Ilse rang.

She said, "Lowree? It is good to hear your voice. You have grown, I bet. It seems so long since I see you. How do things go? We have bad reports of England—of these Trippy people, and much trouble—fighting and such."

"It's not so bad," I said. "You want Pa? I'll call him."

"In one moment. First I talk with you. How is it at school?"

"A bit disorganized."

"But you are doing your work for the examinations? It is important not to lose the *Rhythmus*. . . ."

I didn't see why she had to use a German word instead of the English, *rhythm*. Her accent, her voice altogether, irritated me as much as ever. And I didn't see what right she had to go on about my schoolwork, anyway. She was only pretending to be interested.

I handed over to Pa and went to my room. Andy was there, using my computer. He asked if I minded and I said no, but I thought he could at least have asked first. I tried to read but the key clicks bothered me, so in the end I went down to the living room again. Martha arrived from the kitchen at the same time, for her evening drink.

Pouring it, Pa said, "Ilse sends her love."

"She rang? I wish you'd told me. I'd have liked a word about a plate we picked up in Bath last year. I didn't think my memory *could* get worse, but it does."

"We were cut off. And that was her fifth try at getting through today. The lines are in a mess." He paused. "She told me some things I didn't know: there's no censorship there. In America there's an order for police and troops to shoot anyone Capped on sight—shoot to kill."

"It's time we did the same," Martha said.

"The Swiss think we will, any day now. Listen, Martha . . ."

She looked up from a magazine. "What?"

"Ilse thinks we ought to join her, in Switzerland."

"That's ridiculous. Now the government's finally taking things seriously, this business will be over in no time. It would make more sense for Ilse to come back here. If her father's hung on this long, he's obviously not dying."

They argued for a time, but Martha won. That didn't surprise me—Martha usually did win that sort of argument. And as far as my father was concerned, I felt it was not so much the Trippies that bothered him as Ilse being away. If she came back, it would be as good as us going out there. He said he'd try to get back to her. Martha said it might be a good idea to call the airport first and check seat availability.

He got through to the airport reservations desk fairly quickly, and I heard him ask the position on flights from Geneva. It seemed a routine conversation, but he put the telephone down abruptly.

"Well?" Martha asked.

"Flights to and from Switzerland are suspended."

"It's probably temporary, till things get sorted out."

I could see from Pa's face there was more to it. "The booking clerk said something else as well. Not in any special way, just as a routine remark at the end. He said, 'Hail the Tripod.' "

One of the things I didn't enjoy about sharing a room with Andy was that he woke so early. He didn't make a big performance about getting up, but, in a way, that was worse—half waking and hearing him moving around quietly, carefully closing the door when he went to the bathroom and opening it even more gently when he came back. I'd been awake in the night, thinking about Tripping and the

Caps, and this morning his pussyfooting irritated me more than usual. I was pondering the chances of getting him moved into Martha's spare room, though without much optimism, when he called, "Laur!"

He was by the window.

I said peevishly, "What *is* it?"

"Planes."

I heard the faint roar and ran across the room. We had a good view, and I saw two fighters sweeping in over the hills beyond Todpole. I forgot being annoyed in the pleasure of looking at them, so fast and beautiful compared with the lumbering Tripod. And they, or planes like them, had smashed the Tripods. What did it matter if a few people *were* going around in trances, with power like that on our side?

"Fantastic!" I said.

"More, over there."

He pointed south. A squadron of three were flying towards the first two. Joining up with them, I guessed. I went on thinking that until the rockets started to explode. It didn't last long. One of the two burst into a blossom of orange and red, and the other roared off to the west with the three attackers banking to pursue it.

I said in a whisper, "What's that about?"

But I knew. All five had been Harriers, with air force markings. Which of the sides was Capped and which free I'd no idea, but one thing was certain: military power was divided now, between them and us.

The order came in a radio announcement; television had vanished in a welter of jammed transmissions. All free citizens were to take immediate action to help counter the activities of the Capped. This must involve total cooperation with the armed forces and police, who had authority to restore order by any means at their disposal. The situation was difficult, but could be overcome by free men and women fighting in defense of liberty. Meanwhile, the use of all sea and air routes was confined to government-authorized personnel. As far as possible, people should remain in their homes, avoid using motor transport except for emergencies, and listen for official announcements.

The statement was repeated, and then the frequency our set was tuned to went dead. We found the station again, but it was soon swamped by the grinding buzz of a jammer. The next station we caught was different, with an announcer talking enthusiastically in a Yorkshire accent. Victory for the free people of the world was at hand! All must go forth, prepared to sacrifice everything, their lives if necessary, in the cause. Very soon now we would know the peace and harmony mankind had been vainly seeking since the dawn of history. Hail the Tripod!

Pa and Martha were drinking whiskey. Martha quite often had a drink during the day, but Pa never did, except on holiday. He poured another for them, and said, "It may be grim for a day or two—even a week or two. Food may get difficult." He handed her the drink. "The last word was to stay put. I suppose we have to, but I don't like it."

"Nor do I. Doing as you're told is what takes sheep to the slaughterhouse."

"But there's no alternative, is there? We can't get out of the country. The Trippies have got control of Heathrow, and even if other airports are free, we can't use them now because of the ban on travel. At least we're better off here than in a city."

Martha said, "I've never liked being forced into things."

He said, exasperated, "Does anyone? But you have to face facts."

She emptied her glass. "Face them—and count them. Especially the ones that are on your side. No air or sea travel, from airports or docks, they tell us. If we had a field, and a private plane, no one could stop us leaving the country."

"Since we haven't . . ." He stopped. "You mean—the *Edelweiss*? We'd never get to her. There's probably half a dozen roadblocks between here and the river."

"We'd have to try, to find out."

"But even if we did, and got her to sea, where do we head for?"

"I can think of one place. It's well away from this mess, and I have a house there."

He looked at her without speaking.

In the end, it was I who said, "Guernsey."

Pa said nothing.

Martha asked, "Well? Why not?"

"It's breaking regulations."

"That's what the dog tells the sheep when it steps out of line."

He said, "I suppose if things get nastier in the next day or so—or no better—we could think about it."

"There are times when thinking about something is the worst possible policy." As usual, her voice was firm and decisive. "Let's do it now."

He looked at her a long time, before finally nodding acceptance. "In the morning?"

She put down her glass. "I'll start getting things ready."

When she'd gone, Pa poured himself another drink. He looked at a silver-framed photograph on the sideboard—one of Ilse, laughing, in a summer frock. He'd given way, I realized, because Martha was the stronger character, not because he agreed with her. And perhaps because he didn't want to admit the real reason for not wanting to leave. I thought I knew that, too. It was because this was Ilse's home. Leaving it meant cutting a link with her, possibly the last one.

◎ ◎ ◎
SIX

Martha just told Angela we were going on a holiday to Guernsey; otherwise there would have been trouble about leaving the pony. Andy and I went to the livery stables with her to say good-bye to it. I kept out of the way of its teeth, but it had a go at kicking me which came close. I decided again that I could live comfortably in a world without horses.

All the same, I felt a bit sad watching Angela hugging it. I couldn't take my racing bike, either, but leaving a living thing behind, even a rotten-tempered one like Prince, was different. Though really Prince was going to be all right; it made no difference to a pony who or what ruled the world, as long as the fodder kept coming. Angela fed him his au revoir present of bran mash, and came away cheerfully talking about Guernsey, and whether it was too late in the year for swimming.

We set out at first light in Martha's Jaguar. We were stopped twice by police. They acted tough—hadn't we heard the instructions to stay at home?—but Pa and Martha put on a strong double act. They said she had a sister with a heart condition living by herself at Starcross, who had been panicking on the telephone. The sergeant at the second roadblock asked Pa why he hadn't come alone to pick his aunt up. Pa told him a gang of Capped had been reported close to the village, and he couldn't risk leaving the children or his ailing mother. Martha did her best to look frail; fortunately the light wasn't good.

The sergeant got more friendly after that. He said it was lucky Pa's aunt lived on this side of the river; things were bad on the other bank, and they'd lost contact with Exmouth. There were reports, too, that Capped tanks were on the move from Dartmoor—towards Plymouth probably, but they might swing this way. Pa said we'd get home as soon as possible, and dig in. It couldn't last long, could it?

The sergeant was a tall bony man with a Falklands ribbon.

He said, "My grandfather used to talk about the 1914 War. They told him it would be over by Christmas and he was four years out there." He shook his head. "And at least they could tell who the enemy was."

The weather had turned wintry, and by the time we reached the mooring, just after nine, sleet was driving in from the west. The tide was high—that had been another reason for an early start—and boats jerked and bobbed on their lines. When we left the car's warmth, the wind bit sharply.

We got the rubber dinghy off the roof and put on the outboard.

Pa said, "Laurie and me first, and then I'll leave him in charge of ferrying while I check things inboard. OK?"

Martha stayed behind until last, organizing gear. Andy gave her a hand on board, though she didn't really need it. She didn't move like a grandmother.

She asked Pa, "Everything all right?"

He nodded. "Good job I filled the tanks last time. We don't know who'll be running the filling station."

"I don't suppose you got a forecast?"

"As a matter of fact, I did. A normal weather report, and not a single hail for the Tripod. Cold front passing through with more sleet and rain, snow on high ground. Winds west to southwest, force, five to seven."

"Just as well the tanks are full. Sounds stiff for sail."

They spoke lightly but I realized they weren't relishing the voyage ahead. We would never normally have set out even for a trip along the coast with a prospect of near-gale-force winds.

Martha said, "No point in waiting. I'll get some food going in the galley."

Nothing else was moving on this stretch, not surprisingly, in view of the weather. Sleet drove hard against the glass of the conning deck. Exmouth came up on the port side, a jumble of wet gray roofs. I saw something else—two figures in coast guard oilskins on the jetty. I nudged Pa.

"I know," he said.

One was signaling to us. The other lifted a bull-horn, and a voice boomed across the choppy water, "Come in, *Edelweiss*. Come in, *Edelweiss*."

Pa throttled the engines and we surged ahead, rocking violently. The voice was still shouting, more faintly as we drove out to sea.

Andy said, "Do you think they'll send a cutter after us?"

"I don't know."

Pa felt in his pocket for a cigarette, and then a match. I was surprised he was carrying them—he'd given up smoking a year before. He lit up and drew heavily on it.

"I'd like to tell you a story, Andy—Laurie knows it. Not long after Martha got the Jaguar she took us over to Honiton. It was summer and the main roads were packed, so she used minor roads. They were busy, too, and there was a bend every couple of hundred yards. It was pretty frustrating progress, especially in a car like that. Then, beyond Plymtree, there was a bit of open road with just three cars dawdling ahead of us. She put her foot down. We were doing over eighty when she passed the last of the three and realized what had been keeping the other two back: it was a low-slung police car.

"If I'd been driving I'd have braked and waited to

be pulled up and given a verbal going-over. Martha put her foot right down. They chased her, but she's a good driver and she had the edge, with that engine. She lost them long before Cheriton."

Andy said, "Didn't they do anything about it? They must have got her number."

"Yes. But if you don't have radar, you've got to catch your chicken before you can chop it. They'd have needed to overtake her and flag her down. They could have come round to see her afterwards, but they'd have known her age from the registration details and I don't suppose they fancied lecturing a sixty-year-old woman for outdriving them."

We hit heavier seas, and he eased the throttle.

"The reason I mention it is that I think I'd have been right, then. In a normal law-abiding world it's better to toe the line, and come to heel when the man in uniform calls you. But that world's gone, for the time being at least. From now on it's safer to follow Martha's policy—turn a blind eye and put your foot down."

I said, "No sign of anything coming after us so far."

"Good. Keep your eyes skinned."

Martha had gone below with Angela, who, like Ilse, tended to be seasick even in good weather. I felt my own stomach heaving as we hammered away from the comparative shelter of the shore. I held out for quarter of an hour, and had the satisfaction of seeing Andy dive for the rail before I did. Not long after, Pa handed me the wheel and went to be sick as well. Martha was the only one who seemed unaffected. She brought us mugs of steaming tea, lurching precariously with them across the tilting deck.

Gradually the prospect of pursuit faded; the sea stretched gray and empty all round. Or almost empty—we saw a couple of cargo ships battling their way east and another heading west. Pa observed that trade must drop off when you couldn't guarantee into whose hands a cargo would fall. Time passed slowly, no less slowly for the battering the *Edelweiss* was taking. Martha eventually produced stew, which I ate hungrily and then regretted.

At last there was the long shadow of Alderney on the port horizon, and not long after, Guernsey started to take shape ahead. It seemed an age before we were in the Russell channel, another before we rolled towards the beckoning arms of the harbor.

I felt weak and tired, but cheerful. We'd made it, in lousy weather, and we could relax. I'd always felt safe in Guernsey. Guernsey was different, a place where people drank the Queen's health not as Queen but as Duke of Normandy, because the islands were part of the dukedom which conquered England back in 1066. The mainland, Trippies, and civil war seemed very far away.

Pa throttled back to the four knots which was the harbor speed limit. A uniformed figure watched from the quay, by the harbor master's office.

Pa shouted up to him, "*Edelweiss* from Exeter, visiting. OK for a berth?"

"You can take K3. Know your way?"

"I know my way," Pa said.

"Good. Welcome to Guernsey."

He called out something else which a gust of wind took away. Pa cupped an ear, and he shouted it more loudly.

"Hail the Tripod!"

No one spoke as we chugged in. The harbor was less busy than in summer but otherwise unchanged. In the marina, tall masts swayed in long ranks. A lot of yachts wintered here. Traffic crawled as usual along the front, and the roofs of St. Peter Port rose in tiers behind. Above the crest of the hill the sky was lighter; it looked as though the sun might be breaking through.

When we'd tied up, Pa took us to the forward cabin.

He said, "I had the glasses on people onshore. You can't always tell, obviously, but I'd say at least ten percent are Capped. And the real trouble is the Capped are in charge."

Andy said, "We only know for certain that they're running the harbor."

Pa shook his head. "In an island this size it has to be all or nothing. They've taken over."

Angela said, "Can we go to the cottage? I'm tired."

Her face was white, eyes heavy. I didn't feel all that bright myself.

Martha said, "If they've got Guernsey, I suppose

they must have Jersey as well. But maybe not the smaller islands. There's Alderney and Sark. . . ."

"We'd be pinning ourselves down in a small community. When they do get there—in a few days, perhaps—we'd be sitting ducks."

Martha put an arm round Angela, who was sniffling quietly. "We've not come this far just to give in."

"There's Switzerland."

She said impatiently, "If they've taken over the island, that includes the airport. The no-travel regulation may not apply here: as far as the Trippies are concerned I suppose, the more traveling the better. But they're bound to insist on passengers being Capped."

"Yes, I suppose they will."

Pa went through to the aft cabin. I wasn't surprised he'd brought up Switzerland again. For him, getting back to Ilse was more important than the fight against being Capped. No, that was unfair. But very important.

I was surprised, though, that he'd accepted Martha's argument so easily. I stared up at feet passing along the quay, and wondered if their owners were free or Capped, and, for the hundredth time, what being Capped must feel like. I was thinking miserably that I was likely to find out before long when Pa returned, carrying Uncle Ian's briefcase. He lifted one of the Caps out.

"Basically, it has to be a radio receiver, or something similar. The wiring runs just beneath the rubber. You could snip it with scissors. The Cap would look no different, but it wouldn't receive. So, no induced trance, no compulsion to obey the Tripod."

Andy asked, "Are you sure?"

Pa shook his head. "Not quite sure. But we could try it on one of us, and find out."

I said, "The one who tries it might Trip."

"It would be one against four. We can take it off again, by force if need be." He paused. "I'd volunteer, except that we really want the physically weakest, in case it did come to that."

Angela started crying again; I hadn't realized she was listening, let alone understanding.

Martha said, "Not Angela. Me, if you like."

Andy said, "It's OK. I'll do it."

Pa wasn't looking in my direction, but he hadn't looked at Angela, either.

I said, "I'm next smallest. Let's get it over."

No one spoke while Pa dug the blade of his Swiss Army knife into the inner surface of the rubber. It took time, but eventually he handed me the helmet.

"I've severed it in two places. That should put it out of action."

The thing seemed to writhe in my hands, like a snake. I hadn't looked at it closely before. It was like a flexible skullcap. Even a few days ago I wouldn't have believed that this was something which might take away my freedom of thought and will, but I did now. And now it wasn't easy to believe it could be made harmless so simply. If Pa was wrong and it still worked . . .

I thought of a time when I was about ten, at a pool with a five-meter diving board. Others had dived from it, but when I climbed up the water looked a hundred miles away. I wanted to go back down, but facing the dive was a little less bad than seeing jeering faces. Just a little less. And that had just been physical fear; now I was terrified of losing my mind, my individuality—everything about myself that mattered.

Another thought followed on: what would happen if they did have to pin me down and take the Cap off? Would doing that remove the Tripods' command from my mind? There was no Dr. Monmouth to dehypnotize me. What would they do? Tie and gag me to prevent me raising an alarm? And what if it half worked, leaving me part slave and part free? How long before I went mad?

They were looking at me. If I said any of this, they'd think I was trying to get out of it. They'd be right, too. I thought of the high board, and the heads bobbing in the water. The longer you delayed, the worse it got. I drew breath, and pulled it over my head, dragging it hard down.

Hail the Tripod.

I thought I'd said it, thought in despair that I really had handed myself over to the enemy. I imagined the others had heard it too, and waited for them to grab me. Nothing happened. Could it just have been a random thought? I framed Hail the Tripod in my mind, testing myself with sick anticipation. Then I thought deliberately, I hate the Tripod—and felt a surge of relief.

"Well?" Pa's voice was anxious.

"It's all right." I realized I was shivering. "It doesn't work."

Pa fixed a Cap for himself, and he and I went to the airline ticket office. He asked for five seats on the evening flight to Heathrow. The clerk, who had horn-rimmed spectacles tucked over the flaps of his Cap, punched his keyboard and stared at the screen.

"Five's OK, but you'll have to split up between Smoking and Nonsmoking."

"That's all right." Pa fished a credit card out of his wallet. The clerk shook his head.

"No credit cards."

"What?"

"Not while the emergency's on."

"But you'll take a check?"

"If it's on a local account."

"I don't have a local account. I'm on a boat."

The clerk gave him a knowing smile. "English? I thought you were. No English checks. Sorry. Hail the Tripod."

Pa picked up his card. "Hail the Tripod."

The bank was a few doors away from the airline office. Pa wrote a check and passed it to the teller, who gave it leisurely scrutiny before pushing it back.

"Local accounts only."

Pa said, keeping a reasonable tone, "I don't have a local account. What do I do for money?"

"You could go back to England." The teller rubbed a hand across his forehead and over the Cap. He smiled, too, not pleasantly. "We'll manage without you."

At first, Martha refused to believe it. "This is Guernsey, the friendly isle. *I'll* get local money. The manager at Barclay's knows me. He's been cashing checks for me for over twenty years."

Pa said, "You don't understand, Martha. It's all changed. If he's manager still, he must be Capped. And arguing might make him suspicious about your Cap working properly. It's not just a local rule, but a total change of attitude."

"But why? Why should being Capped turn people against foreigners?"

"I don't know, but it must be something that suits the Tripods. They could be thinking on the same lines as Julius Caesar with the Gauls: divide and rule. Maybe if they win we'll wind up all living in villages, instead of cities. It would make it easier to keep us under control."

That was the first time I'd heard anyone suggest we might lose. Angela said, *"Can't* we go to the cottage?" She sounded frightened, as well as tired.

Martha said sharply, "They're not going to win, whoever or whatever they are. How much money do we need for the tickets?"

"Three hundred would cover it. But . . ."

She produced a leather bag and rummaged, bringing out jewelry—gold bangles, necklaces, rings.

"One thing about the antiques trade is that it teaches you the value of portable capital. I'll get the money."

Pa said, "I'll come with you."

She shook her head firmly and reached for one of the Caps. "No, you won't. I haggle best on my own."

Two airlines flew between Guernsey and England. Pa tried the other next, in case the first booking clerk was curious about the way he'd found a means of paying. This one took the pile of local notes without query and booked us on the last flight out.

Before we left the *Edelweiss,* Pa fixed the remaining Cap for Andy. There wasn't one for Angela, but he assumed they wouldn't bother about young children. I looked back at the boat as we climbed the steps at the end of the pontoon—one more thing to leave behind. Whatever lay ahead, apart from what was left of Martha's jewelry, we were going into it stripped.

The weather had cleared, and the late afternoon was lit by watery sunshine. The taxi took us up the hill leading out of St. Peter Port, and I recognized familiar landmarks. In the past they'd been part of the excitement of coming on holiday, of anticipating the long days of sea and sunshine. On the left in Queen's Road was the entrance to Government

House. Something new stood beside the gate—a wooden model of a hemisphere supported on three spindly legs. I couldn't read the lettering underneath, but I knew what it would say.

We checked in early, and Martha took us to the airport restaurant. She told us to order whatever we liked; the money left over after the tickets were bought wasn't going to be any use outside the island. She and Pa ordered champagne.

While the waitress was opening it, a man at another table said, "Mrs. Cordray, is it not?"

The back-to-front white collar under the black Cap showed he was a clergyman, and I recognized him as vicar of the parish where Martha's cottage was. He'd visited when we'd been staying there.

Looking at the champagne, he said, "Something to celebrate?"

"My birthday." She smiled convincingly. "Will you have a glass?"

He did, and they chatted. He'd always been a great talker. In the past, though, he'd seemed anxious to please; now he was sharp, almost aggressive. He asked if we were going back to England, and when Martha said yes he was approving, but in an almost contemptuous tone.

"Much better, I'm sure. England for the English, Guernsey for the Guernseyman. Things are going to be better in all sorts of ways. My mother used to talk of life in the island in the war, during the German occupation: no motorcars, no tourists. Thanks to the

91

Tripods, it can be like that again. In their blessed shade, we shall find peace."

"Do you think they're going to come back?" Pa asked.

The vicar looked surprised.

"The Tripods, I mean."

"But they are back! Didn't you hear the news on Radio Guernsey? There have been new landings all over the world. So now they can complete their mission of helping mankind save itself from war and sin."

Martha said, "No, we didn't know. Is there one in the island?"

"Not yet. It is something to wait and hope for. Like the Second Coming." His voice was thick and earnest. "Indeed, perhaps it *is* that."

The first throw of the dice was when they called the flight. For as long as I could remember, there had been security checks because of terrorists. Pa had said checks would be unnecessary with everyone Capped, and he proved right. We weren't even screened for metal. We walked through to the departure lounge and almost immediately after that across the tarmac to the aircraft.

They were using a Shorts plane, with just pilot and copilot and two stewardesses. The aircraft took off normally, heading west, and when he'd gained sufficient height the pilot banked for the northeasterly flight to England.

For us it was the wrong direction; each mile flown would have to be retraced. Moreover, not knowing the fuel load, every gallon or half gallon might be crucial. Pa got up and walked towards the forward toilet. The stewardesses were at the rear, fixing coffee. Andy and I gave him time to reach the door to the flight deck before following.

This was the second part of the gamble: would the door be unlocked? Pa turned the handle and threw it open. As the copilot turned to look, Pa pushed through and I went in behind him, blocking the doorway. He pulled Martha's pistol from inside his jacket, and said, "I'm taking over. Do as I say, and everything will be all right."

I had the fear, for a moment, certainty, that we'd got it wrong. In the old pattern, the hijackers had been nutters and the aircrew sane; this time it was the other way about. Being Capped, the pilot would do not what he thought right, but what he thought the Tripods wanted. If the Tripods wanted him to crash the plane, with himself and forty passengers on board, he wouldn't hesitate.

Both men were staring at the pistol. The pilot said, "What do you want me to do?"

"Set a course for Geneva."

He hesitated for what seemed a long time. The hope was that, seeing us wearing Caps, he'd have no reason to think we were anti-Tripod. Finally, he shrugged.

"OK. Geneva it is."

© © ©
SEVEN

The pilot, Michael Hardy, took being hi-
jacked more easily than I would have expected. He
asked Pa why he was doing it, and Pa told him it was
because his wife was in Switzerland, and flights there
had been suspended. It struck me as a fairly crazy
reason, but Hardy accepted it with a nod. I guessed
that one of the effects of being Capped could be to
make people generally less curious. The stewardesses
and the passengers didn't seem bothered about what
was happening, either. The Cap probably worked as
a tranquilizer as well.

Just how unconcerned the pilot was became clear
after he'd fed details of the new flight path into his
computer.

He yawned, and said, "Should just about do
it."

Pa asked him, "What do you mean, 'just about'?"

"Fuel. We've enough for Geneva, but there won't

94

be anything over for a diversion. Let's hope we stay lucky with the weather."

One of the stewardesses brought us all coffee, and he talked as we drank it. Flying had been something he'd always wanted to do. As a schoolboy, living near Gatwick airport, he'd spent most of his spare time plane spotting. Until recently, he'd thought of his present job as a stopgap; his ambition was to fly the big trans-Atlantic planes.

Munching a biscuit, he said, "Funny that, looking back. I mean, why bother?"

Pa said, "You're happy now to stay on the local run?"

Hardy paused before answering. "I've spent years ferrying people around the sky at hundreds of miles an hour. What's the point? They'd be just as happy where they are. Happier. My wife's got a share in a farm, and I think I'd rather help out with that than fly. People don't need airplanes, or cars and trains for that matter. Do you know what I *would* like? A horse and trap. I'd really like that."

He did another computer reading in midflight, which showed fuel was lower than predicted.

"Getting towards touch and go," he said casually. "Paris would be easier."

Pa didn't answer right away. I wondered if he was waiting for Hardy to add something, or reconsidering the situation. Geneva meant Ilse for him, and escape from the Tripods for all of us. It also might mean taking a chance on the lives of everyone on the plane.

95

"We stick with Geneva," he said at last.

Hardy nodded. "OK, Geneva. Let's hope this head wind gets no worse."

No more was said. I started remembering all the movies about air crashes I'd seen. One time at Andy's house, his mother had talked about her fear of flying. She wouldn't go anywhere if she had to travel by plane. I'd thought it weird at the time, but I didn't now. We were up here in this metal tube, miles high, and if the fuel ran out, our chances of survival were just about nil. I visualized the petrol tanks emptying, second by second, and began to sweat.

I thought, too, of what Hardy had said of his feelings since being Capped. He seemed happy. And if the Tripods really were bringing peace, surely that was a good thing? Peace was about people liking one another; and perhaps in a way that meant they didn't get hooked on one particular person and forget about others.

Moonlight provided a hazy view of snow-covered mountains, and Hardy started the landing procedure. That didn't improve matters; if anything it made them worse. As the undercarriage went down, one of the engines coughed, picked up again, then sputtered into silence. I was really terrified now. I shut my eyes as the landing lights appeared in front, and they were still shut when the wheels bumped down onto the tarmac. I felt suddenly weak with relief.

Hardy taxied the plane to a standstill close to the

terminal building, and I found something else to worry about. The airport authorities knew about the hijack, of course, but we had no idea what their reaction to it was going to be. All the communications with flight control had been formal, concerned with getting the plane down. It seemed a long time before the doors were opened, and we were ordered to disembark. I could see Pa chewing his lip.

I'd thought they might separate us from the crew and the rest of the passengers, but after Pa had handed Martha's gun over we were all taken through the arrival area to a smaller lounge, where there were soldiers with automatic rifles.

A senior officer said, "You will please remove the Caps from your heads."

Captain Hardy said, "No. That's impossible."

"At once."

Hardy said, "I ask permission to refuel and take my plane and passengers back to Guernsey."

"Permission not granted. Take off Caps."

We four had pulled the helmets off our heads, but none of the others made a move. The officer barked a command in German, and two soldiers advanced on Hardy.

He backed away as they approached, and shouted to the officer, "You have no right to touch us! I insist you give us petrol and clearance to return."

The officer ignored him, and the soldiers kept coming forward. The vicar who had talked to Martha in Guernsey was standing close by.

He stretched out his arms and said, "We bring you peace. Put down your weapons, and accept this blessing." He made a gesture, of three downward strokes, with his right hand. "In the name of the Tripod."

As the soldiers grabbed his arms, Hardy went berserk, tearing himself free and punching one of them in the face. The rest of the Capped rushed forward, screaming.

I heard Martha's voice, above the din. "Quickly! This way—"

We made for the door through which we'd entered. Two soldiers raised their automatics. Pa said, "We're not Capped. Look."

He tossed his on the ground; but they still kept their weapons trained on us. Behind, the screaming was punctuated by a single shot, and then by a rattle of automatic fire. I looked back to see a couple of the Capped on the floor. Captain Hardy, blood pouring from a wound in his neck, was one.

It was quickly over. Shocked into silence, the rest stared dumbly at the soldiers, two of whom took hold of a man about sixty, and pulled him to one side. He started to cry as one of them tore off his Cap, and went on crying as they moved on to their next target. It was a dreadful noise, which got worse as others had their Caps forcibly removed. They offered no further resistance, but it was like listening to animals being tortured.

The officer in charge came to us.

"You will be escorted to the debriefing room."
His voice was cold. "Obey all orders."

Pa said, "We damaged the Caps so they wouldn't work. We've not been under Tripod influence."

The clipped voice did not change.

"Obey orders."

They interviewed us separately, and at length. Eventually we were given food, and taken to a hotel for the night. When Pa asked to be allowed to telephone Ilse, he was refused. There was a telephone in the bedroom he shared with Andy and me, but it wasn't connected.

Next morning Pa and Martha were interviewed again, and after that we were taken before a stiff little man with a black beard, who told us we'd been granted permission to stay in the country for seven days. We were free to travel to Fernohr, but must report to the police as soon as we got there. He pushed across a piece of paper which was our authorization.

Pa said, "And after seven days?"

"The position will be reconsidered. You are aliens who have entered this country illegally. You would be returned to England, except there are no flights at present. I must warn you that any failure to obey police instructions will result in immediate deportation for all, to any country which will accept you."

"Can we keep the Caps we were wearing—the ones that don't work?"

"Why?"

"In case we need them again."

"There are no Tripods in Switzerland, so you will not need them." He shrugged. "It has been established that they are harmless. Keep them if you wish."

Martha sold more gold to get Swiss money, and we took a train to Interlaken. The track ran beside the lake, which stretched as far as the eye could see. The day had started cloudy but now both sky and lake were clear and blue, with just a few clouds over the mountain peaks on the far side. Pa had a relaxed look. There was plenty to relax from—the hijack, fear of the plane crashing, and then the business at the airport. Things were different in real life from television—the gunshots more deafening, the blood brighter red and spurting horribly.

As I was thinking there was also, for him, the prospect of being with Ilse again, he said to Angela, "We'll see *Mutti* in a few hours. I wonder if she'll recognize us after all this time."

"Of course she will," Angela said. She was eating an apple. "It's not that long."

Martha was looking out of the window. Between us and the lake there were houses, with children playing, a frisking dog, smoke rising from a chimney.

She said, "It has a nice safe look. Do you think we'll be given that extension?"

Pa stretched. "I'm sure of it. You get the bureaucrats at airports. Local police are different."

The train stopped at Lausanne, where the time-table scheduled a thirty-minute wait.

I asked Pa, "Can Andy and I have a look around? We'll be back in plenty of time."

"Better not, just in case."

I thought quickly. "I'd like to see if there's something I can get as a present for Ilse. It's her birthday next week." Angela wasn't the only one who could play that sort of game.

He hesitated, but said, "All right. As long as you're back in a quarter of an hour."

Martha said, "I don't think you'll be able to buy anything with English money."

"I was wondering if you'd change some for me?"

"And how long before I'm able to use what I change?" She smiled and fished in her wallet. "But I suppose I asked for that. Twenty francs—it'll have to be something small. You'd better have a bit to spend, too, Andy."

Angela said, "And me."

I said, "No. You stay here."

"If you're going, I can." Her eye had a steely look. "It isn't fair if you get a present and I can't. She's my mother!"

I argued, but didn't expect to win. Martha gave her twenty francs as well, and she tagged after us while we explored the station. We found a little shop, and I wondered whether to get Ilse chocolate, or a doll in peasant dress. While I was deciding, Angela bought one of the dolls, so it had to be chocolate. There were two sizes, at nine francs and nineteen. I asked for the smaller, then changed my mind and picked the other.

I'd been vaguely aware of people gathering near us. The voice immediately behind startled me. *"Sales Anglais!"* I knew that was French for "dirty English," but if I hadn't, the tone of voice would have given me a good idea.

He was about sixteen, tall and dark-skinned, wearing a red jersey with a big white cross, the Swiss national emblem. There were others with similar jerseys in a mob of a dozen or more, mostly about his age but a couple younger, and one man with a gray beard who looked about fifty. Those that didn't have jerseys wore red headbands with white crosses.

Andy said quietly, "Let's get out of here." He moved towards the platform, but the tall boy blocked his path.

Another, shorter and fair-haired, said, "What are you doing in our land, filthy English?"

Andy said, "Nothing. Going back to the train."

Someone else said, "Filthy English on clean Swiss train is not good."

"Look," Andy said. "That's twice we've been called filthy English." He'd raised his voice. "The next one gets hit."

There was silence for some moments. I thought he'd got away with it, and Andy must have, too. He pushed forward against the tall boy, forcing him to give ground. A gap in their ranks opened, but only for a second. One grabbed his arm and swung him

102

round; another kicked his leg viciously, bringing him down.

As he fell, Angela screamed. I caught her arm and pulled her in the opposite direction. They were concentrating on Andy, and it looked as though I might succeed in getting her away, but Angela yelled again and I saw the man with the beard grabbing her from the other side.

After that there was confusion in which I kicked and punched at shapes around me and got kicked and punched in return. One blow to the neck made me stagger and struggle desperately to keep on my feet. I'd had a glimpse of Andy on the ground, grunting as they kicked him.

I had my arms over my face, trying to protect myself. There was shouting, mixed up with the boom of a loudspeaker announcing trains. I realized the punching had stopped, but flinched as someone seized me roughly. I opened my eyes to see a gray-uniformed policeman. Two others were lifting Andy, and the red jerseys were scattering into the crowd.

Angela seemed unharmed. Andy was bleeding from the mouth, and there was a cut over one eye and another on his cheek. When I asked him how he felt, he said, "No sweat. I'll live. I think."

The police escorted us back to the train. I told Pa what had happened, while Martha cleaned Andy up. The police demanded details of our journey, and checked passports.

103

During the scrutinizing, Pa asked, "What are you going to do about them?"

"These children are your responsibility," the senior policeman said. He had a round face and small eyes, and spoke English slowly but well. "You have permission to proceed to Fernohr. Report to local police on arriving."

"I wasn't talking about these children." Pa was chewing his lip again. "The ones who attacked them—what are you doing about *them*?"

"We do not know their identities."

"Did you make any attempt to find out?"

"And we do not know if there was provocation."

"Provocation! The children were buying presents for their mother—who happens to be Swiss—when they were called filthy English and set upon. I thought this was a civilized country."

The policeman cocked his head, small eyes staring.

"Listen, Englishman. This *is* a civilized country. And a country for Swiss people. We do not need foreigners here. Do you wish to make a complaint?"

Martha said, "Forget it, Martin."

The policeman rocked on his heels. "If you wish to make a complaint, you must leave the train and come with me to police headquarters. You will stay there until my superintendent is free to see you, and discuss this complaint. I do not know how long that will be, because he is a busy man. Well, Englishman?"

Pa said, tight-voiced, "No complaint."

"Good. Make sure that no one of your party causes more trouble. I wish you a safe and swift journey—back to England."

As the train started, Pa said, "I don't understand it."

Martha said, "I never did like the Swiss." She added, "Apart from Ilse, of course."

Andy said, "I did say I'd hit anyone who called us dirty English again. That's when they came at us. I'm sorry if it caused the trouble, but I didn't see how I could have just listened and said nothing."

"No," Pa said. "I know what you mean. But we may have to do just that—listen and say nothing—in future. It's a different kind of xenophobia from the brand we found in Guernsey, but it's still xenophobia."

Angela asked, "What's zenner-foe-be-ar?"

"Fear of foreigners. Fear and hatred. It can be valuable, protection for the tribe, and it can also be nasty. It's a funny thing. On the surface what we saw in Guernsey seems better—people just wanting to be left alone to live their own lives—while here it's aggressive: a positive urge to attack foreigners. But this one's healthier. The Swiss have wrapped themselves up in being Swiss and hating anyone who isn't. It's tough on us, but it may be a good protection against the Tripods."

He and Martha went on talking about it as the train picked up speed. We could see the lake again, flat, calm and peaceful, with two or three small boats

105

and an old-fashioned paddle steamer making stately progress towards Geneva. I was thinking of my part in the proceedings. I'd tried to get Angela away because she was a girl (and my half sister) and needed protecting. That had also meant leaving Andy to the mob; I hoped he understood why. One eye was nearly closed from the swelling round it. He saw me looking, and winked with the good one.

Pa had telephoned Ilse from Geneva, and when the train stopped at Interlaken she was on the platform. She kissed Martha and hugged Angela, but her eyes over Angela's shoulder were on Pa. Then she and he moved towards one another slowly. She put her hands out, and his hands took them. They stood close together, smiling, for some moments before he kissed her.

It was Ilse who eventually broke away. She was smiling and crying at the same time. She turned from my father to look at me.

"Lowree," she said. "Oh, Lowree, I cannot say how good it is seeing you again."

She came towards me, and I put my hand out.

"Good seeing you, too."

It was funny. I'd put my hand out so she wouldn't kiss me, and I hadn't thought I meant it about being glad to see her. But in a way I was.

◎ ◎ ◎
EIGHT

Fernohr was a little mountain village, built round a single road with a wooded slope above it on one side and a staggering view down into a valley on the other. The road from Interlaken ended there, or practically ended. It continued up the hillside as an unpaved track, giving access to half a dozen dwellings, and finally to the Gasthaus Rutzecke.

The first Rutzecke house had been built by Ilse's grandfather as a vacation spot for the family, but between the world wars her father rebuilt it on a larger scale, as a guesthouse. It had eight bedrooms and a couple of lounges, and a terrace in front where there was a telescope and a pole flying the Swiss flag.

The Swigram had stopped operating it as a guesthouse when the Swigramp got ill. The only person living there apart from family was a handyman called Yone, even older than the Swigramp. He also looked after the animals—chickens and two cows that ambled round the sloping meadows with bells round their necks—and shot game for the pot. He had an old shotgun he tended lovingly.

The Swigram was white-haired and plump. She spoke little English, and seemed a bit in awe of Pa and more so of Martha, who spoke to her kindly but rather in the way she'd spoken to the daily help back home.

There was snow the second day, but it thawed almost immediately. Ilse said it was warm for the time of year. I looked longingly at the rack of skis in one of the sheds, and meanwhile Andy and I explored around. The terrain was fairly dull above the chalet, cropped grass and boulders, but more interesting below the village, where there were pine woods and some good climbs. The lake was visible down in the valley, and we could watch boats crossing, through the telescope. It was coin-operated, but the box was open; so you just put the same twenty-centime piece through over and over again.

We also helped Yone with the chickens and cows. The chickens sometimes laid astray, and we had to hunt for the eggs. And the cows had to be found and brought in at night. I tried to talk him into letting me use the shotgun, but he wouldn't. It wasn't a wildly exciting life, but pleasant enough. The Swigram was a better cook than Martha, too.

Her husband, the Swigramp, lay all day in the big double bed in their bedroom, except in really good weather when she and Yone moved him into a day-bed on the balcony. I sat with him sometimes but never knew what to say, and he didn't talk either. But he always smiled when Angela came into the room. I didn't know if he had any idea what had brought us here, or if he even knew about the Tripods.

Swiss radio and television were in French and German; Ilse had to tell us what they said was happening in the outside world. It seemed that in most places the Capped were now in charge, but the Swiss weren't worried. For hundreds of years they'd been surrounded by dictatorships and empires and such, and had managed to disregard them. They had the protection of their mountains, and an army in which all male citizens served. The Tripods were a nuisance, but so had Napoleon and Hitler been. They felt all they needed to do was sit tight and go on being Swiss.

They were taking some precautions. They'd rounded up their local Trippies at the beginning and put them into camps under armed guard. The few who had escaped the original sweep and tried to distribute Caps were quickly caught and imprisoned. Ilse, who had only seen things from the Swiss viewpoint, was sure the Tripod craze would soon die away. Pa wasn't so optimistic, but hoped the Swiss might be able to cut themselves off from the rest of the world, as an oasis of freedom.

In the village we at first encountered similar antiforeign feelings to those in Geneva and Lausanne. The villagers made a point of ignoring us, and the shopkeepers—there was a combined dairy-bakery, and a general store—were surly and unhelpful. When it came to renewing our permit, the village policeman, a man called Graz, hesitated a long time. In the end he said he would stamp a renewal only because we were related to the Rutzeckes: the Swigramp was well known and respected.

Some of the local boys carried things further, and followed us, chanting insults. One of the leaders was Rudi Graz, the policeman's son. He was only thirteen but well built, and he picked on Andy in particular.

The third time it happened, when we were leaving the village on our way back to the gasthaus, Andy stopped and turned round. The Swiss boys stopped, too, but Rudi said something in the local dialect, and the rest laughed. Andy walked back to him and spoke one of the few German words he knew: *Dummkopf,* meaning "idiot."

The fight lasted about five minutes. Andy was cooler and a better boxer, but Rudi was a hitter and got some nasty punches in. One opened the cut over Andy's eye, and he bled quite a lot. It was Rudi, though, who eventually stood back. They looked at one another, and after a moment Andy put a hand out. The Swiss boy ignored it and turned away, his mates following. It didn't make them any friendlier, but they stopped chanting after that.

Angela sometimes insisted on coming with us to

the village, and she sometimes did get a smile, I suppose because she was a little girl and pretty.

She also made friends with an old horse, which had been retired from the Swiss Army and grazed in a field not far from the bakery. One day, after she'd stroked and talked to it, she said, "He's a bit like Prince. Don't you think so, Laurie?"

I said warily, "A bit, I suppose."

"What's going to happen—about Prince?"

"Nothing. I mean, they'll look after him at the stables until we get back."

She swung round to stare at me, her blue eyes scornful.

"But we're not going back, are we? They're only saying that."

I wasn't sure what would come next—whether we'd have weeps—so I jabbered about not really knowing what was going to happen but everything coming right eventually.

When I'd ground to a halt, she said, "I wake in the night sometimes, dreaming I'm Tripping again. Though in a way it's worse—I know what's happening, and hate it, but can't do anything to stop it. When I wake up properly, at first I'm scared, and then . . . I can't really say how it is. Just, well, feeling good. Feeling safe."

She pulled a tuft of grass, and the horse nibbled it from her hand.

She said, "I hope Prince *is* all right."

I said, "I'm sure he is."

She looked at me again. "But you don't have to

111

pretend. I don't want to go back there—not even for Prince."

We'd never before talked about anything serious—as I knew this was. And I knew she was being brave, as well as a lot more grown-up than I'd realized. I felt awkward, but wanted to let her know I understood that. We weren't a family that went in for hugging, but I put an arm round her, even though Andy was with us.

I said, "Come on. The Swigram's waiting for the bread."

Everything changed suddenly when French and German armies invaded Switzerland without warning. One day the village was in a frenzy of excitement over the news, the next, deserted-looking, with all the men between eighteen and sixty called to the colors.

The attitudes of those that remained changed, too, perhaps because their hatred was now concentrated on the invading armies. They smiled at us and were even prepared to chat. And they were full of confidence.

Frau Stitzenbahr, the baker's wife, whose two sons had gone, said, "It is terrible, this, but not for long, I think. French and Germans are fighting always. Swiss men do not wish fighting, but they are brave and love our land. They will chase the French and Germans quickly home."

Andy and I walked back up to the gasthaus. It was a gray, cold afternoon. Although the snow still held off here, the surrounding peaks were whiter from fresh falls.

I said, "Lucky Pa's not Swiss or I suppose he'd have had to go, too. What do you think's going to happen?"

The path overlooked a drop. Andy threw a stone, and we saw it bounce off scree hundreds of meters below.

He said, "The Swiss think being patriotic makes them a match for anyone. They don't understand what it's like facing an enemy that's Capped."

"Those at the airport surrendered as soon as the army began firing."

"That was different. Why should the Tripods care about a tiny group like that? It didn't matter what happened to them. But now they're sending in armies—armies of men who don't give a toss about being killed."

I thought about it—fighting and not minding if you got killed. You'd have to be Capped to feel like that. "Anyway," I said, "I shouldn't think the fighting will get as far as Fernohr."

Nor did it. And Frau Stitzenbahr was right, it was finished quickly. But not in the way she'd thought. Next day there were reports of retreats in the north and west, and by the following morning it was over. Ilse translated the news on the radio: everlasting peace had come to Switzerland as it had already to the rest of the world. The next bit even I could understand.

"*Heil dem Dreibeiner!*"

Two days later, looking through the telescope, I saw the familiar shape of the paddle steamer, furrowing a path across gray waters towards Interlaken. And something else, scuttling monstrously along the shore. I called out Pa and Andy.

When Pa had looked, I said, "There's nowhere else to go, is there?"

Pa looked weary, and his chin had a stubble of beard, black with patches of gray. In the past he'd always shaved as soon as he got up. He shook his head, without answering.

We gazed down the fall of land towards the lake. You could see it, though less clearly, with the naked eye, lurching across farmland, not caring where it trod, or on what. Pa's face had an expression of despairing misery. I hadn't realized that misery maybe got worse the older you were.

I said, "We're pretty remote, though, aren't we? They may not come up here."

He shook his head again, slowly, as if the effort was painful. "Maybe not."

Martha and Angela came out, too. Martha was watching Pa rather than the Tripod; after a time she said in a more gentle voice than usual, "Ilse's with the Swigramp—he's not so good this morning. Why don't you go and sit with her?"

Over the next few days the men straggled back to Fernohr. There hadn't been many casualties because the fighting had lasted such a short time. And then

114

one morning, on the way to pick up the day's bread, we saw that the villagers were wearing Caps.

I whispered to Andy, "What do we do? Get out fast?"

"It might draw attention. Look, there's Rudi. He's not Capped."

We'd learned in Guernsey that people weren't Capped under the age of about fourteen, probably because young children weren't regarded as a threat. It seemed likely the same rule applied here. Rudi was a year younger than we were, so Angela was safe, but Andy and I could be at risk. We walked on, trying to look casual. In the baker's shop, Herr Stitzenbahr was bringing in trays of fresh loaves from the bakery, and Frau Stitzenbahr, behind the counter, offered her usual greeting of *"Grüss Gott."* It was all normal, but for one thing: the black Caps covering her braided white hair and his bald head.

Frau Stitzenbahr asked about the Swigramp and went on chatting while I ached to get away. At last we had the loaves and our change, and could leave. We headed up the village street, but within fifty meters met a group of men strolling down. One of them was Rudi's father.

He didn't look like a policeman. He was small and thin, with an unhealthy, sallow complexion. He had a policeman's manner, though. He stood in front of us, blocking our path.

"So, die englischen Kinder . . ." He looked at me closely. *"Wie alt? Vierzehn doch?"* He translated it

laboriously: "How old, boy? Have you yet fourteen years?"

So fourteen *was* the Capping age. I said earnestly, "No, sir. Not till next year."

"You must bring certification of birth." He frowned. "It must come from England. This is unsatisfactory."

Unsatisfactory for him, maybe. With a lift in spirits, I realized it was something that could be played along, maybe for months. Still frowning, he turned to Andy.

"But you are already fourteen. This is certain."

"No, sir," Andy said. "Thirteen and a half."

In fact he was only two months older than I was, but with two inches advantage in height and his grown-up look he could have passed for fifteen. Rudi's father shook his head.

"I do not believe this. It is necessary you are Capped. Today Caps are finished, but tomorrow the mail van brings more. You will have one."

Andy nodded. "If you say so, sir. I'll come back in the morning."

"No. You will stay here. There are some foolish ones who do not wish the Capping. You will stay here, boy, till new Caps are come."

Andy tugged the hair at the back of his head, something he did when he was making his mind up. One of the other men, who happened to be the local wrestling champion, moved closer. Andy sighed.

"Whatever you say." He looked at me. "You'll tell them what's keeping me?"

116

"Yes. I'll tell Pa." I gave him a thumbs-up sign. "No sweat. It's going to be all right."

Angela and I watched him walk away with Rudi's father in the direction of the policeman's house. I tried to tell myself there was a chance he might escape on his own, but didn't believe it. He'd need help. The first priority was to get back to Pa and tell him.

On the outskirts of the village we met Rudi. To my surprise he stopped, and spoke. "Why is Andy not with you?"

I saw no reason not to tell him, and had a feeling the news wasn't a surprise. His father had probably talked about the English and Capping. But he didn't look as pleased as I would have expected. He resembled his mother rather than his father in being big and blond, and like her he usually had a big empty smile. He wasn't smiling now.

"He must stay, for the Capping?"

I nodded.

"Does he wish this?"

"I don't know." I got cautious. "But it has to happen, doesn't it—to everyone?"

He said slowly, "They say so."

We found Pa and Martha in the residents' lounge at the front of the gasthaus, drinking coffee. They were talking but stopped as we came in.

Angela burst out with the story, and I let her tell it.

When she'd finished, Martha said, "That's terrible." She paused. "But the Caps won't arrive till to-morrow? I'm sure he'll manage to get away before then. Andy's resourceful."

I said, "There's a room at the police house like a cell. Yone told us. It's got a bolt and double locks, and the only window is ten feet up and barred. It's not a question of being resourceful. He *can't* get away without help."

She shook her head. "I wish there was something we could do."

"We have to."

"You don't understand." She looked tired and angry, and her face had that stubborn look adults have when they're not going to listen to you. "We can't."

I said, trying to be patient, "But we must."

Martha said, "Yone told us about the Caps while you were gone. He met someone he knew with one. We've been discussing what to do. We can't stay here, so close to the village. It will only be a matter of days before they come to Cap us."

"As far as Andy's concerned, it's not days, it's to-morrow morning."

She disregarded that. "Your father and Yone have a plan. You know the rail tunnel up to Jung-fraujoch?"

I nodded. It was a trip I'd taken the first time I visited Switzerland. The track was on the far side of a deep valley separating Fernohr from the lower slopes of the Eiger. The train climbed through a tunnel ac-

118

tually inside the mountain, taking nearly three hours to reach the terminus station, three and a half thousand meters above sea level, where there was a hotel and ski station and an astronomical observatory.

"The hotel and the line are closed, because of the emergency," Martha said. "Yone says we could hide inside the tunnel. We'd have protection from weather, and there may be food in the hotel. It would do for the time being, at least. Better than staying and being Capped."

"Sounds great," I said. "I'm totally for it. As soon as we get Andy back."

Her face tightened into still angrier lines, which meant she was feeling guilty.

"We can't. For one thing, we need time. Yone wants to make another reconnoitering trip before we all go. There's something else, too. The Swigramp's dying. He may last a couple of hours, or a couple of days, no more."

"I don't see what difference that makes. If he's dying, he's dying."

She said harshly, "Probably you don't. At your age." I suppose putting me down helped. "But it makes a difference to the Swigram, and Ilse. We can't take him with us, and they won't go while he's still alive. We need those few days' grace. If we try to rescue Andy, we'd be stirring up a hornet's nest, whichever way it turned out. They'd be swarming here right away."

119

She saw my face, and said in a quieter voice, "I'm sorry. I like Andy."

"What if it were me?" I asked. Martha didn't answer. "Or Angela?"

I turned to my father, who hadn't spoken so far.

"We're not going to let him down, are we? He told me to let you know what had happened. And I said, 'It'll be all right. I'll tell Pa.' "

He didn't look me in the eye. He said, "I'm sorry, too. But Martha's right. We don't have a choice."

Halfway to the village I stopped. A sense of my own stupidity hit me almost like a solid weight. Stupidity and ingratitude. I thought of all Pa had done to get us away from the Tripods—crossing to Guernsey, the hijack, bringing us here. And now he had this new plan to keep us safe. What made me think I knew better than he did?

Martha was right, too: a rescue attempt that went wrong would put everyone at risk, which also applied to my idea of going it alone. Even if Pa was prepared to abandon me rather than endanger Ilse and the others, I was still likely to draw attention to the people in the gasthaus.

I was aware of thinking it out, of being clear-headed, cool, rational. It was early evening, suddenly cold, with the mountains outlined sharply against a sky that was dark blue above, yellow in the west where the sun had gone down. A jay croaked, out of sight, probably looking for a late snack.

120

And I became aware of something else, behind the thinking out part. Nothing cool this time, but a feeling of relief so great I wanted to yell it to the silent mountain. I'd known I was scared of going back into the village, but I hadn't realized how scared. Utterly terrified, in fact—even more frightened than I'd been when the plane was trying to get into Geneva.

I stood looking down at the huddled roofs of the village, with smoke rising almost straight from their chimneys. It was a picturesque and ordinary scene, except that the people beneath the roofs had lost what lay at the heart of being human: their individuality, and the power to act as free men and women. But in their case it had been forcibly taken from them; I was surrendering mine out of cowardice.

And I remembered what Pa had said, about Martha and the police car. There were times when all you could do was put your foot down hard on the accelerator, and take your chance. I knew the answer to the question I'd put to myself on the plane, as to whether it wasn't better being Capped and alive than being dead. I took a deep breath of the frosty mountain air and started off downhill again.

◎ ◎ ◎
NINE

It was dark by the time I reached the village; night came fast in the mountains. My first objective was to find out about the conditions in which Andy was being held, and I decided a direct approach was best. I'd told Martha I was going to my room to read, and had taken a couple of books from the lounge as evidence. They were in my hand as I pressed the brass bell-push outside the policeman's house.

Footsteps sounded heavily inside, and I braced myself to confront Rudi's father. But it was his mother who opened the door. She looked at me in surprise.

"*Ach, so. Der Engländer . . . Was willst du?*"

"Something to read." I showed her the books. "For my friend, Andy."

She said something I didn't catch. I shook my

head, and she spoke in English. "You give books me so I give your friend?"

That was no help. I asked, "Can I see him?"

She shook her head doubtfully. I heard Rudi's voice behind her. They had a rapid conversation, and at the end she motioned me to come in.

Rudi said to me, "You cannot see Andy until my father says yes. He is gone to the inn, but back soon. You will wait?"

At least I was inside the house, though not too hopeful of getting further. There was no reason really why I shouldn't just leave the books, which was what I was fairly sure Rudi's father was going to tell me to do.

Despite being dubious about letting me in, Frau Graz produced a jug of homemade lemonade and a chocolate cake. She gave Rudi a piece, too. His homework lay open on a table.

I nodded towards it, and said, "Don't let me stop you."

He shrugged. "It is *Naturwissenschaft.* Science, you say? And we end this study soon."

"End? Why?"

"The chief teacher tells us *Naturwissenschaft* is not needed anymore. There is no need to learn science now that Tripods rule."

I could see the reason. Science was a part of independent thinking, and that was over for the human race.

I looked at Rudi. I knew practically nothing about

him, but he'd looked worried when we spoke about Andy being Capped. And this was a situation where one had to take chances. His mother was in the kitchen, humming to music from the radio.

I said quietly, "They say the Tripods are our friends—that everything they do is for our good. What do you think?"

He paused. If I'd got it wrong, he would probably report me to his father, which would fix things properly.

But he said at last, "Andy does not wish the Cap?"

I'd gone too far to draw back.

I said, "No. Nor do I. Do you?"

He took a deep breath. "No, I do not wish it. I hate the Cap!"

There was no problem, Rudi said, about releasing Andy; his father kept duplicate keys in his study. He left the room, and came back with a key which he handed to me.

He said, "To the left, past the back door. I will talk with my mother while you do this."

It was a kind of shed, but solidly built. I unlocked the door and found a room furnished only with a metal trundle bed. Andy was on his feet as the door opened.

I said quickly, "No time to talk. Rudi's keeping an eye on his mother. Let's go."

He said "Right," unhesitatingly. I felt good as he followed me through the yard. Pa had said there was

124

nothing we could do, but I'd done it. It didn't hurt either that this time Andy was doing the following.

Rudi came from the kitchen, calling something back reassuringly. We went through the hall on tiptoe. There was a stuffed bear, guarding an umbrella stand; though moth-eaten, it looked ready to pounce. I pushed a fist into its ribs, and saw dust rise.

Rudi opened the front door a crack, and looked out warily. I was impatient for him to open it fully. Instead he stood back. He looked at me helplessly.

The door was opened from the other side, and Rudi's father came in. He was wearing his uniform. I thought how much a part of it the Cap seemed.

He took in the scene, and said sharply: *"Was heisst das?"*

Rudi just stood there. I didn't know what to do either.

Andy said, "Run for it. Now!"

He charged Rudi's father, knocking him off balance. As Graz shouted, I got past, but looking back saw that he'd recovered and was holding Rudi. He shouted again, and I saw figures running along the street towards us. Andy was wrestling Graz, trying to free Rudi. I went to help, but Graz's reinforcements were on us. In a matter of moments we were bundled back inside the house.

We'd been unlucky, as Rudi explained later. Normally his father went to the inn, had a few steins of beer with his cronies, and came back alone. This time, after he'd talked about the English boy he'd taken into custody, the group had discussed it and come to the conclusion that it was unwise to take chances, especially with a foreigner. The English boy should be Capped right away, and one of those who already had a Cap should surrender it for the purpose. They'd followed Graz back to the house with that in view.

There were five, including Rudi's father. They restarted their discussion, but it was soon clear they had a problem. They were all agreed on the importance of Andy being Capped, but which of them was to give up his Cap? As they argued, it emerged that no one was willing. Like the people at the airport, they found the thought of being without the Cap intolerable—even temporarily, and even to serve the interests of the Tripods. In the end they reluctantly decided Graz had been right in the first place, and they should wait till the new Caps came in the morning. It was also decided that Rudi and I should be Capped along with Andy.

We were given extra mattresses, and blankets. Frau Graz came in and fussed over Rudi, but didn't seem bothered about his being locked up; I wondered if that was due to the Cap, or to being Swiss and married to a policeman. When she left I prowled around, looking for means of escape.

Andy said, "I've checked. No go."

"You couldn't reach the window," I said, "but if I stood on your back, I could."

Rudi shook his head. "This will not work. All win-

dows of the house have electric—how do you say—
Alarm?"

"Alarm," Andy said. "I don't think we can do anything tonight. Did you say they'll take us to the
church to be Capped?"

"Yes. It is *Zeremonie.* Big show."

"We might have a chance of making a break then.
Meanwhile better grab some sleep. I was here first so
I get the bed."

Andy settled down, and as far as I could tell went
to sleep right away. I lay on my mattress, brooding. I
didn't know whether Andy had anything particular
in mind in talking of making a break, and I didn't
see we stood a chance anyway, with the entire village
against us.

How could he, or anyone, sleep, faced with the
prospect of being Capped? I felt I mustn't waste any
of the moments in which my thoughts were still free,
and tried to stay awake. But sleep came nevertheless,
and in fact I slept heavily. The small square of window was bright when I was wakened by the cell door
being unlocked.

The mail van from Interlaken was due to arrive
about nine, and we were to be Capped immediately
after that. Frau Graz produced a large breakfast, and
though I thought I wouldn't be able to eat, the smell
of ham and eggs convinced me otherwise. She was
quite pleased Rudi was to be Capped in advance of
his birthday, and told us how much better for it we
would all feel. Her sister, Hedwig, who suffered

127

from depression, had cheered up as soon as she put the Cap on, and her own rheumatism had been much less painful.

She broke off to answer the door. On the kitchen wall a pendulum clock of dark wood painted with flowers indicated eight thirty. Graz and another man were in the room with us. I was again aware how hopeless our chances were. Then I recognized the voice speaking to Frau Graz. I stood up quickly as she came back, with Pa following her.

He was wearing one of the Caps we'd used in the hijack.

He looked at me sternly, and said to Graz, "I am sorry to hear my son has behaved badly. I will take him home and punish him."

Herr Graz shifted comfortably in his seat. "It is not necessary. He will be Capped this morning. After that he will not do wrong things."

"He should be punished," Pa said. "It is my right, as his father."

After a pause, Graz said, "A father has rights, that is true. You can beat him if you wish."

Pa glanced at Andy. "This other is also in my care. I will punish him, too."

Graz nodded. "That is permitted."

"So I'll take them both back to the gasthaus."

Graz raised his hand. "No. You shall beat them here. Outside in the yard. I have a strap you can use."

I wasn't surprised it hadn't worked. Like my effort with the books, it was a bit thin. But I was sure Pa

128

would have something else to fall back on. I sat there almost smugly, waiting for him to produce an argument which would flatten this stupid Swiss policeman. I was shattered when he finally did speak.

"All right. But I will get my own strap."

He turned away, not looking at me. I couldn't believe he was leaving us.

I called after him, "We're being Capped this morning. Soon."

He went out without answering, and I heard the front door close. Frau Graz bustled up, offering us rolls and cherry jam and more coffee, while her husband loaded a nasty-smelling pipe. The other man yawned and picked his teeth. I couldn't look at Andy.

If he'd not come at all, it wouldn't have been so bad. I'd let myself in for this and must take the consequences. But he *had* come, with that feeble excuse about punishing us, and then given in and left when Graz called his bluff. He was going back to the gasthaus, to Ilse and Angela. He'd protect them, all right. I felt as I'd done the time he came out to play football, and I kicked his shins. Only worse; this time I knew I hated him.

I went so far as to think of a way of getting even, a better way than kicking. All I had to do was tell Graz about the fake Caps. The Tripods could have him, too, and Ilse, and Angela—everyone. I started to say it: "Herr Graz . . ." He looked up from his pipe.

"What is it, boy?"

I shook my head, feeling sick. "Nothing."

It seemed a long time before the doorbell rang again, though in fact it was only minutes. Frau Graz went to answer it, sighing with exasperation. When I heard Pa's voice, and even when he came into the kitchen, I felt numb. I wasn't going to start hoping again. I didn't even look at him, until Graz gave a grunt of surprise and dropped his pipe with a clatter on the table.

Frau Graz stood by the kitchen door, looking agitated. Yone was there, too; and Pa was holding Yone's shotgun.

As a good Swiss housewife, Frau Graz kept a pile of clean tea towels in a cupboard beside the sink, and they came in handy as gags. She thought this was a robbery—it made no sense to her that anyone should use force to prevent someone being Capped—and started gabbling about where the family valuables were kept. I gagged her into silence, avoiding her reproachful looks. Pa and Yone had dealt with the men, and Pa approached Rudi.

I said, "No. He helped us. He doesn't want to be Capped, either."

"We can't take chances. If the alarm's raised—"

"Rudi," I said, "tell him you want to come with us."

"Yes." He nodded. "Please. I hate the Cap."

"It's too risky."

I didn't want to argue. I felt bad about the way I'd felt when he went to get Yone. But I couldn't accept this decision any more than the one over Andy.

I said flatly, "You've got to let him come."

Pa looked at me. He shrugged, with a little smile. "All right. *You* keep an eye on him."

As we left the house, a passing villager exchanged greetings with Yone. I wondered how long we had before an alarm was raised. Less than half an hour, certainly. If Graz wasn't there to meet the mail van, they would come looking for him.

We squeezed into the Suzuki, and Pa drove off, revving hard. We found Ilse outside the gasthaus, struggling with a bulging backpack, and Martha came out with another. Ilse's face was blotchy, as though she'd been crying.

Martha said, "You've got them."

She tried to make it sound ordinary, but there was a tremor in her voice as she looked at Pa. She'd always bossed him, but he was her son, as I was his. She wiped her face with the sleeve of her dress. "We're just about ready."

I remembered the other reason for wanting more time and asked, "What about the Swigramp?"

Pa took the pack from Ilse, and heaved on the strap. Over his shoulder he said, "He died, in the night."

I looked down into the valley. People still died; the Tripods and Capping made no difference to that. And others had to go on. Far below I could see a section of the road that wound upwards from Inter- laken. A yellow spot was crawling there: the mail van was on its way.

The first part of the route led higher up the mountain by way of a rough track, which deteriorated and eventually disappeared. It wasn't easy going, in places very hard. Martha and Ilse tackled it well, but the Swigram was soon gasping and we were forced to slow down. We lost sight of the gasthaus, and for a time our only view was of the steeply climbing rocky slope and an ominous gray sky beyond. The wind was northeast, razor-edged. Yone thought there would be snow before nightfall.

A halt was called where there was a patch of level ground. The gasthaus was once more in view, and Yone pointed down. There were three cars outside the house, apart from the Suzuki. Pa scanned the scene with field glasses which had belonged to the Swigramp.

When I had a chance to look, I found they were so heavy it wasn't easy to hold them steady, but the magnification was good. I recognized Graz. There were seven or eight men altogether.

Smoke rose from the gasthaus chimney, as it did all the year round—even in summer the big wood-burning range was in use, for cooking. But the smoke looked thicker than usual and was coming not only from the chimney but one of the bedroom windows as well.

Fire wastes no time in sweeping through a wooden building, and in seconds we could all see it. I heard the Swigram moan as the smoke's blackness was shot with flame.

132

Holding her mother, Ilse said to Pa, "Why? To destruct a house like that . . . only because we refuse the Caps?"

"I don't know," Pa said. "To prevent us going back there, perhaps. To discourage anyone else from defying the Tripods. One thing we can be sure of: neither pity nor mercy are going to come into it. They believe what the Tripods tell them, and as far as the Tripods are concerned we are nothing but a nuisance. Like rats."

Andy said, "I read somewhere that by trying to kill them, men have actually improved the intelligence of rats."

"Yes," Pa said, "I read that, too. Rats have lived close to man for thousands of years. Every one we managed to kill improved the breeding stock, because the brighter rats survived and reproduced. Maybe we're going to have to take a leaf out of their book."

Ilse said, "They must have found his body." She was speaking of the Swigramp. "But they did not bring it out, for burial."

"No." She still had an arm round her mother, and he put his out to embrace them both. "But it doesn't matter, does it? It was his home for nearly sixty years. No one could want a better funeral pyre."

We resumed our trek. Having led exhaustingly upwards, the route changed to lead down even more steeply. It was wild, jagged country, with no sign of human beings or anything connected with them. We saw a group of chamois, the local deer, leaping from crag to crag, and an eagle soared close to one of the crags above.

The Swigram needed to rest a lot. Pa and Yone, and then Andy and I, took turns helping to support her. She apologized for the trouble, and said we should leave her.

Pa said, "Just take it slowly, *Mutti*. We have plenty of time. And no one's going to leave you. We can't spare you. We can't spare anyone. There are too few of us."

At last we reached a more gentle slope and could see the little railway station of Kleine Scheidegg, the last stop for the cogwheel train before it entered the tunnel. As Yone had predicted, it was deserted. Tourism was a thing of the past, along with parliaments and television chat shows, universities and churches, human disorder and human freedom. The station shop, which had sold chocolate and maps and silly souvenirs, was boarded up, and the last train stood unmanned and covered with snow.

At this altitude there was deep-packed snow all round, and the tail of a glacier close to the tunnel mouth. It was late afternoon. The sky was a deepening melancholy gray, the whole landscape barren and wretched. As we toiled up the last few hundred meters it began to snow, in huge relentless flakes. I felt cold and miserable and hopeless.

134

◎ ◎ ◎
TEN

I found the notebooks in which I'm writing this in the hotel; they were order books used by the restaurant manager, some partly filled with lists—*20 kg Blumenkohl, 1 Kiste Kaffee, 45 kg Kartoffeln*—"cauliflower, coffee and potatoes"—that sort of thing.

That was about a week after coming here. I'd thought the journey through the tunnel by train tedious, but it was much more so on foot. It was nearly five hours before Pa's flashlight lit up the platform sign, JUNGFRAUJOCH. Minutes later we stepped out into a dazzling landscape of snow and ice, with the frozen river of a glacier stretched into hazy distance, surrounded by high white peaks. All was empty and lifeless: no animals, no birds, not even an insect. But no people, either, except for ourselves . . . and no Tripods. We stood on the cold roof of the world, rulers—for what it was worth—of all we surveyed.

The purpose of this journey through the tunnel

was to see if provisions had been left here, and we struck lucky. The hotel had kept good reserve stocks, apparently against the possibility of the rail line being blocked in winter. There were shelves loaded with cans, bags of flour and sugar, beans and dried fruits and rice. There were even deep-freeze cabinets whose contents, because of the below-zero temperature at this altitude, had stayed frozen after the electricity supply was cut off.

Flashlights and batteries were an important find. We only had two from the gasthaus, which we'd had to keep switching on and off to conserve power, and there were enough in the hotel, in vacuum-sealed packs, to last years. We found candles and oil lamps, too, and drums of fuel.

In a siding at the station there was a diesel coach with a charged battery, and after Pa had experimented with the controls we loaded it for the return journey. While he and Yone were making final checks, I showed Andy some of the things I'd seen when I was there before, including a room filled with ice statues. He was fascinated by a life-size ice motorcar, and pointed out it must have been carved more than seventy years ago because it was a model of an early Ford. I thought of how much things like motorcars and airplanes had changed in those seventy years. It was as though mankind had been a surfboarder, riding a high wave of invention. Who could tell what wonders might still have lain ahead? But now, thanks to the Tripods, it had all ended.

During the winter we gradually adjusted to our new life. Although the nearest house was more than ten miles away down the mountain, and the tunnel entrance commanded a good view of the approaches, we took care to leave no traces and to avoid creating recognizable paths in going out and returning. Yone instructed us in this, and kept a close watch to make sure no one slipped up.

He also instructed us in the use of the skis we took from the hotel ski school. Despite having looked forward to it, I found skiing very difficult to begin with—the sense of losing contact with the earth bothered me—and had plenty of falls. I spent ten days immobilized with a strained thigh muscle. Andy took to it much more quickly, and Rudi, of course, was an experienced skier: I watched him skim down the slopes below the tunnel mouth with admiring frustration. But I slowly got the hang of things, and then found it more exhilarating than anything I'd known.

At the outset we ventured out primarily for recreation—confinement in the tunnel was oppressive—but with the coming of spring we launched more purposeful expeditions. With snow and ice surrounding us all year long, water was never going to be a problem, but Pa decided we should aim at conserving food supplies.

I said, "But there's enough in the hotel to last years!"

Martha asked, "How many years?"

I saw her drawn face in the lamplight and realized fully for the first time that this was no temporary resting place—that she at least expected to end her days here. The Swigram did die, before spring came, not from any particular sickness, perhaps just from missing the Swigramp. We wrapped her body in a blanket and lowered it into a crevasse in the glacier, covering it with snow. We could not mark the grave, but her body would lie there forever unchanged in the perpetual frost. A different end from the Swigramp, whose body had burned to ash in the flames that destroyed the home they'd shared, but bodies didn't matter, really. They had both died free.

So we started expeditions to get food. We aimed at isolated houses, traveling long distances to find suitable targets. In some cases we were able to raid larders or take hens or eggs while the owners slept. But there were times when people wakened and had to be intimidated by the sight of Yone's shotgun. Fortunately so far we've not had to use it.

It's theft, of course—we have no money to leave if we wanted to—but the people we steal from are Capped, and we are as much at war with them as their Tripod masters. On the third expedition we found an un-Capped girl in the house, and stole her, too. She was dubious at first, but eventually agreed to come with us. Her name is Hanna. She's a few months younger than I am, and has yellow hair that's beginning to darken. Her eyebrows are dark already, her eyes deep brown. She speaks English in a husky voice and with a German accent, but it doesn't irritate me the way Ilse's once did.

I find myself getting on with Ilse better all the

time. It's difficult to remember how much she used to madden me in England. (I was going to write *at home,* but remembered that this is the only home we now have, or are likely to have.) She took over the cooking from the Swigram and although not as good yet, is improving. And of course, the Swigram didn't have to cook with limited supplies on a primitive oil stove stuck in a tunnel.

On one expedition we found a man living alone, and Pa tried the experiment of removing his Cap. We had to overpower him, and he cried pitifully afterwards. But when we left he followed, and Pa let him join us. His name is Karl, and he's in his middle twenties. Although physically strong, he can only do simple things, under instruction. At times you find him crying, for no apparent reason. We don't know whether his mind has always been slow, or if it happened because we removed the Cap. But it's something we agreed we would not do again.

And in fact we couldn't if we wanted to. In late summer a Tripod came to the valley, and stationed itself close by a village called Karaman. From a vantage point we watched what followed. All day long a procession of Capped came to stand by the Tripod's foot. A tentacle lifted them one by one into the belly of the machine, and after some minutes deposited them back on the ground. Through field glasses we could see that in place of the black of the helmets, their heads gleamed silver when they were put down.

It was Andy's guess that this could signify the replacement of the original Caps with something more permanent, and he was proved right when, on our next trip, we found a man and woman, both silver-headed. The horrifying thing was that the silver part was a metal mesh, which seemed welded into the living flesh. From now on, the Cap, once imposed, was there for life, and eventually would crown a skeleton.

That was when Pa decided to adopt a deliberate policy of recruiting young people who were likely to be Capped within the year. We take none by force, though that would be justifiable with such an alternative. For our own security we can't afford to harbor doubters. And so far, of five given the chance, only one, a boy called Hans, has chosen to accept. It is obviously not easy to leave parents, and the comforts of home, to join an unknown band of marauders, but it's depressing that so few are willing.

It seems to me that boys are more ready to take the risk than girls. Two of the four who refused were boys, and both seemed to hesitate, whereas the girls were quite definite about it.

I said something of the sort to Angela, and had my head snapped off. *She* was as willing to take a risk as any boy, she said, and it was unfair Pa still refused to let her go on the scouting trips. For that matter, what about Hanna, who'd been the first to join us? In fact, she pointed out, the score was equal between boys and girls as far as recruits went.

"Hanna's different," I said.

"Oh yes, isn't she?" she said scornfully. "Because

you fancy her. Well, you're not likely to impress her talking that way."

I ended the conversation by walking off to my private patch of tunnel, thinking there were times when Angela really was insufferable. She was growing up, of course—she'd had her eighth birthday just before we left England, and her ninth was not far off. I had to admit she was bright, though—a bit brighter, if I were honest, than I'd been at her age. And though her pertness sometimes drove me mad, I reflected, as I cooled down, that in general I found her, too, easier to get on with these days. I made up my mind to organize a trip to the hotel to find a birthday present. I remembered seeing a mirror in one of the rooms which she might like.

Autumn brought snow again, and an end to the days of lying out in the sunshine that burned so fiercely through the thin air. Once more we took to skis and darted across the white untrodden slopes. And one day, above Karaman, we watched a Tripod pass beneath us. This time it did not stop by the village but crawled on, disappearing round high ground to the east. Just over a week later we saw it again, and Pa looked at his watch.

"The same time, within minutes. I wonder if it's a routine patrol?"

Over subsequent weeks, we studied the Tripod. It *was* a patrol, and one carried out with monotonous regularity. Every fourth day the Tripod passed below our aerie shortly before eleven in the morning, treading a path that varied as little as the time.

On the fifth occasion we saw it, Pa said, "I wonder what the object is? I suppose, just keeping a general watch over things."

He wiped away tears with the back of his glove; there was a biting northeast wind, and his eyes were inclined to water.

Andy said, "The way it thumps along, it could set off an avalanche."

That was something Yone had recently warned us about. The mountain slopes were packed with snow, and an incautious movement could trigger off disaster. He had been a survivor of an avalanche as a young man—he was dug out of a cabin after days of being buried—and he'd described the horror of it: thousands of tons of snow and rock hurtling down with the speed of an express train and the noise of ten.

Pa said, "Pity it doesn't."

Something occurred to me. "I wonder . . ."

Pa wiped more tears away. "What?"

"We know it arrives here at the same time, every fourth day." I looked down the slopes immediately beneath us, heavy with new snow. "What would happen if someone fired a shotgun into that, just as the Tripod was passing underneath?"

Yone, who suffered from rheumatism which sometimes crippled him for days, had not been with us that morning. He closed his eyes, listening to what Pa said.

142

"It is possible. But not easy to say when avalanche is—ripe, is it? And not easy to guess path it takes."

"But worth trying?"

Yone paused before replying. "We take care no one finds us, make no tracks. But if we try, and it not work, perhaps they will come look for us."

It was something to consider. The Tripods themselves, unwieldy as they were, could not invade our mountain fastness, but they had silver-headed slaves at their disposal in virtually endless numbers. If in failing we showed our hand, they could use them to track us down. And once they did, though we might defend the tunnel entrance for a time, our fate was certain.

For days we argued the question. Martha and Ilse were vehemently against the idea, Yone more calmly opposed. Most of the younger ones were for it, with varying enthusiasm. Angela demanded to be one of the party carrying out the attack. For my part, I thought what Yone had said made sense. I could imagine what it would be like being trapped and besieged in the tunnel. Our present life was not too bad, and you could say we were making progress. With the spring we could start recruiting again. The sensible thing was not to take a risk that might destroy us.

But being sensible wasn't enough. The hatred I felt for the Tripods and what they had done to us was too great. Nor could I abide the thought of huddling here forever like moles, while our enemy

143

stomped arrogantly through the valley. I wanted to attack!

Next morning Pa called us together in that part of the cave which was our general meeting place. Oil lamps hung from hooks which Yone had screwed into the rocky ceiling, and an oil stove provided smelly warmth.

He had with him a battery-powered radio we'd found at the hotel, powerful and with six shortwave bands. At the beginning it had been possible to pick up occasional faint voices on it, sometimes too faint for the language to be distinguished. But the voices had died, one by one. It was months since anyone had bothered to listen.

He said, "I stayed up last night, searching the air waves. Nothing but Tripod buzz."

He was referring to the radio sounds we assumed came from the Tripods, an oscillating noise that didn't seem to have any coherent pattern.

"That doesn't mean there aren't free men out there. There may be groups without transmitters, or afraid to use them for fear of being traced. But we have to act as though we're on our own, now and for the foreseeable future. We must act, that is, as though we're the last hope of the human race."

He stopped and wiped his brow; I saw he was sweating, though it was not all that warm. I looked from his face to Martha's, Ilse's, Yone's. Yone was the only one who seemed unchanged, but he'd always looked ancient. All the rest showed new signs of strain and tiredness. It was easier, I realized, for

144

people of my age to adjust to confinement and hardships, and the lack of comforts, than for old people like them.

"What this means," Pa went on, "is that everything we do is critical. Our first aim has to be self-preservation, but self-preservation isn't enough. Aiming just at that, we could slip into a routine of caution and playing safe which would progressively weaken us, and eventually destroy us as totally as the Tripods have destroyed our cities. So our second aim must be to fight the Tripods—without much hope for the immediate future, but as a means of keeping hope alive.

"That's why we go out to recruit the young—why we've brought in Hanna and Hans and, God willing, will find more." He wiped his face again. "And that's why I think we must attack this Tripod, even if it means risking our own destruction. My personal instinct is to leave well alone, play safe. Martha and Ilse and Yone feel the same way. But we're old and overcautious. The young are for attack, and the young are right."

Ilse said, "No! Martin, you must listen. . . ."

Pa looked at her with a grim face. "I lead this group. I never saw myself as a leader, but there it is; in a situation like this, someone has to. And a leader has to command confidence, and consent. I hope I will always get your consent to things I propose, but if ever I don't you will need to choose someone else."

A silence followed. Everyone knew there was no

145

one who could take his place. Eventually, when he was too old, someone would, but that was a long time in the future. Maybe Andy, I thought, looking at him across the cave. I looked at Hanna, with the lamplight shining on her hair. Or maybe me. A lot of things had changed, not just in the world outside but in me, to make that believable.

"The day after tomorrow," Pa said. "That's when the Tripod's due again."

The party consisted of Pa, Andy, and myself. Yone had given us a further warning. Our aim was to start an avalanche below us, but there were slopes above which were also overcharged with snow. The shock might start another, higher up, that could overwhelm us. Setting out, Pa said if we didn't come back the others were to take orders from Martha. He kissed Ilse, holding her a long time.

She came to me then, and said, "Take care, Lowree."

She was looking at me, and there was a tear on her cheek. She made no move towards me, but I went forward, and kissed her, too. "I will."

We moved into position on a clear morning, with sunlight sparkling from the peaks and the surface of the lake below. Then came the waiting—only for an hour, but seeming much longer. At one point, on a slope to the west of us, a minor shift of snow looked as though it might be the start of a natural avalanche, but as we held our breaths the slide checked, and all was still again.

146

Pa looked at his watch for the hundredth time. At that moment, following the same path round a spur of rock as it had on previous occasions, the Tripod came in view, three or four hundred meters below us and more than twice that to the west. Now Pa faced the crucial problem of judging the moment to fire Yone's shotgun.

Rising to his feet, he pointed it at the snow slope. The Tripod was coming on in its awkward skittering motion, a metal spider that had lost all but three of its legs. From up here it looked small, unthreatening.

How deceptive that was! Across the valley to the north we looked at a wasteland of white peaks, but beyond them lay what had been great cities. And the simple reality of this metal beast, stalking unchallenged through a remote alpine valley, was the measure of our humiliation. I thought back to the early days, and Wild Bill talking about Close Encounters of the Absurd Kind. Whatever bizarre creatures had launched the Tripods, no one had taken them seriously until it was too late.

No, not too late. I wouldn't accept that. As long as even a handful of men and women survived free, hope lived. And Pa was right: we must risk everything to fight them, for without fighting, everything was lost.

I saw his finger crook in the trigger guard. It was too early! The Tripod was a hundred meters short of the point the avalanche would hit. I wanted to cry out, tell him to hold fire. . . . Then the shotgun went off, its thunder shattering the still cold air.

. . . And nothing happened. The snow remained even, undisturbed. Below, the Tripod continued on its twisting way. Pa fired the second barrel, and thunder reverberated again. I heard Andy whisper, "Move! For God's sake, move!" Then slowly, very slowly, the surface rippled, and the snow started to slide.

It gathered speed only gradually, moving at a child's walking pace to begin with. That was when I felt sure that, instead of firing too soon, Pa had left it too late. The Tripod came steadily on, varying neither pace nor path. It would be past by the time the wave of snow arrived. I felt like weeping with anger and despair.

"Go on! Go on!"

That was Pa. I heard myself echoing him—"Go, go!"—as though urging the mountain, the planet which had borne us, to come to our aid. We were all three crying out, shouting for help to the empty sky.

And the avalanche was gathering force, spreading, foaming up out of itself, tossing huge boulders into the air as though they were specks of gravel. It looked as though the whole face of the mountain was on the move. The sound, as Yone had said, was titanic, a thousand giants bellowing wrath. Faster and faster it drove, then suddenly seemed to leap and charge forward like a living thing . . . and sweep over the Tripod, burying it. When the avalanche finally came to a halt, an unbroken expanse of snow lay beneath us.

148

At the beginning of summer I sat outside the cave with Andy and Rudi. We are a united company—we have to be, the way we live—but I get on better with them than with Hans, or Dieter, the boy we recruited just before Christmas. I like Hanna better still, but that's a different story; not really to do with sitting and idly talking.

We were talking about the Tripods and the avalanche. For weeks after, we waited in apprehension, expecting reprisal or at least response. There was none. We kept constant patrols, but nothing happened, and no new Tripod came.

Then, with the melting of the snow, a patrol—unfortunately I was not on it—witnessed a strange sight. Two Tripods crawled along the valley and approached the spot where the hemisphere of the wrecked one was just beginning to be visible. They probed around it with their tentacles for several minutes, then went back the way they had come. As they disappeared, the wreck erupted in a fount of flame.

I had been arguing that the two must have come in response to some kind of radio beacon. Andy shook his head and said, "Doesn't make sense. Why wait all that time? They must have known something was wrong when it didn't return to base."

"Knowing something's gone wrong isn't the same as knowing *where* it's gone wrong. Their transmitter was probably blocked through being under snow. Then, when the snow melted—"

"All they had to do was send another Tripod

along the same route to look for it. They didn't."

"How do we know that? We weren't able to keep watch all the time."

He paused, but when I thought he'd yielded the point, said, "Because the second Tripod would have left thumping great tracks in the snow, wouldn't it? I should have thought that was obvious."

Rudi said, while I was trying to think of an answer, "I think they are knowing from the beginning."

I asked shortly, "Why?"

"Because they do not take time looking at the wreck. All they do is explode it."

"So why wait all those months?" Andy came in. "Why not do whatever they were going to do right away?"

Rudi shrugged. "I do not know. All we truly know is how little we know of them. What matters is that now they send no Tripods through the valley. It is not much, but it is better."

His calmness calmed me. What he said was right. We had managed to destroy one Tripod, and in this small corner of the world, none had replaced it. I remembered the speculation about their coming from a swamp world. Perhaps mountains were unfamiliar to them, and perhaps they would decide they were dangerous and keep away from them in future. It was a small victory, but something to build on.

No one spoke for several moments. The sun

150

scorched overhead. Around us the green grass was studded with a dozen different colors of summer flowers, and above, against a strong blue sky, a pair of yellow butterflies slowly waltzed. A lazy day—the sort of day for a game of tennis, a bike ride, fishing maybe . . . then back home to a shower, tea, television. . . .

Andy said, "I like the idea of this extended patrol Martin was talking about."

They all called Pa Martin these days, though certainly not from lack of respect. Everyone listened carefully when he spoke. But he talked to me more than the others, and I called him Pa.

Rudi said, "Yes. We will make more recruits if we go further."

And yet what a lot there was to build! I could see no end in our lifetimes, perhaps not in centuries. At least, though, we'd made a start. I wondered about those who would come after—if maybe one day three like us would lie on this hillside in the sun, watching butterflies as we were doing, but able also to look towards a day which would see humanity free again.

Our job—my job—was to lay the foundations which could make it happen.